The Story of Everything

Eric S. Schrock

RIVERSONG
BOOKS

An Imprint of Sulis International Press
Los Angeles | London

THE STORY OF EVERYTHING

ISBN (print): 978-1-946849-76-2
ISBN (eBook): 978-1-946849-77-9

Published by Riversong Books
An Imprint of Sulis International
Los Angeles | London

www.sulisinternational.com

Contents

To Ruth, Joshua, and Ela

So that you might see God as I do

Note from the Author

I never set out to write a book. I set out to study the Bible. As I studied the Bible, I found a cord woven throughout its pages that tied everything together. That cord became this book. This cord that ties everything together is not original with me, but, I believe, designed by God Himself. Too many people have dismissed the Bible as an ancient book filled with a collection of stories, much like *Aesop's Fables* or *Grimm's Fairy Tales*. Some believe the Bible to be a collection of moral stories while others dismiss it as myths and fairytales. The Bible does contain stories, most of it is narrative in nature, but it is not a collection of stories. It is one story. Penned by multiple people over a great period of time, it tells the singular, spectacular story of God.

So why write this book? While some may look to a study guide or other analytical material to help them understand the nature of God, I believe that stories are the most effective way to communicate truth. As a preacher and public speaker, I can feel an audience fall asleep as I drone on about some theological point. That same audience stirs to life when I tell a story that illustrates the same point. You may argue that speaks more to my oratory skills, and I gladly concede the point, but Jesus also chose to use stories when He taught. He used stories to teach profound truths and those lessons continue to be repeated to great effect even to this day. People of all ages are drawn to stories. This is why we are drawn to television and movies. We enjoy the stories that are told.

I believe God must enjoy stories. That's why He designed us to enjoy them so much. Reader, I have written this book, so that you might enjoy the story within. I pray that this story helps you understand the nature of God. Perhaps along the way, we can learn more about ourselves as well.

This book found its inception in a Bible study with my friend and fellow missionary, Kolt Mackrill. Over gallons of coffee and countless meetings at Starbucks, the basic outline of this story took form. As iron sharpens iron, I thank him for being the one that sharpened me. Thanks for your input and your friendship. This book would be nothing more than an idea without your help. And thank you, Amy, for letting me borrow your husband.

I'm sorry I never asked if I could write a book. Lili, your patience with me and your love for me drives me to be a better man. Thank you for bearing with me while I sat at the computer writing this book. You are the one that keeps me and my book grounded in reality.

My first and favorite reader is my daughter, Ruth. Your eager anticipation for each new chapter drove me to write more and better. You made all *the difference*. I pray that your faith remains firmly grounded in the Bible and that your voice sings out forever toward heaven.

I also wish to thank Dr. Melody Harper. It was in your class on Orality that God refined my thinking and approach to the story of everything. This book is the project I wish I could have turned in for your class. Continue to push your students to proclaim God through story.

A special thanks also goes to Moisés Silva. This side of heaven we may never understand the nature of choice, but your insight helped me to refine how it was presented in this book. Thank you.

The English language can be difficult, especially without an editor. I am thankful God blessed me with a wonderful editor, Debby Drust. Not only did you help me to put all my commas in place, you also challenged me to write better. The cultural and character development that you encouraged are welcome additions that improve the feel of the book.

Finally, I wish to thank my parents. You were the first to teach me about God. I strive to follow in your footsteps.

Eric Schrock
May 19, 2020
Sfântu Gheorghe, România

Chapter 1

Beginning

"I don't understand why you won't let me go with my friends. Just because it's the Sabbath back in Jerusalem doesn't mean it is here. None of my friends celebrate the Sabbath. Besides, I'm only half Jew. Please, *Immah*. I just want to go. *Papà* would have let me go."

Eunice looked at her son. When did he get so tall? He looked exactly like his father, if only a bit thinner and not quite as tall. Timothy had the same dark hair, strong jawline, and prominent nose of the man she missed so much. Now was no time to mourn, though. How should she answer her son? She knew it wouldn't be long before Timothy would stop asking her permission. How could she make him understand? Sacrificing his Jewish heritage and faith to the more popular ideas of his Greek friends would cost him more than he could know. *Help me*, she prayed silently.

"It's not about being Jewish or Greek, Timothy. But for the record, your best half came from me. So be careful what you say!" she added with a smile. As she began preparations for the evening meal, she continued, "It's about our faith in God. The Greek gods your friends all worship are merely idols that people have created to please themselves. We worship the one true God not because we made Him, but because He made us."

"I know, I know. I've heard all the stories. *Sabta* has made sure of that. But what do the stories of Adam and Eve have to do with me and my friends now?" Timothy pleaded.

"Oh, now you don't like my stories?" came the quick, soft voice of Lois as she entered the room. No longer able to move with the speed of her youth, her small, frail body betrayed the quick, strong mind of Timothy's grandmother. Yet, even the ravages of time and disease could not diminish the smile from her face.

"That's not what I meant! *Sabta*, you know I love to listen to your stories. It's just that *Immah* won't let me go out tonight with my friends."

"Help me over to my chair and then maybe I'll help you with your mother." Timothy crossed the room to his grandmother and lent his arm. As she leaned on him, she added, "Of course, I might help your mother, she is my favorite daughter after all."

"Oh, *Sabta*, she's your only daughter, but I'm your only grandson. How will you ever choose which side to take?" Timothy said with a smile. He helped the old woman into her chair then covered her with a blanket. Even though the weather was warm, he knew she would appreciate the gesture. Maybe she would side with him.

"Perhaps I should side with my handsome young grandson after all," said Lois with a quick glance to her daughter. Eunice was busy chopping vegetables but shook a quick "no" with her head. "I think, perhaps, I should just tell you another story. One that I've never told you before."

"*Sabta*, you've told me all the stories a dozen times, from Adam to Abraham to David to the prophets. I know each one of them, the same as I know my name and the same as I know you're my favorite grandmother."

Lois chuckled at the blatant attempt to gain her favor, then adjusted the blanket in her lap and began, "No, you're right,

Timothy. For a situation like this, no ordinary story will do. No, you are a young man, more man than a child, yet you still need direction and wisdom. In a time like this, we must go back to the Scriptures, to the Word of God. My dear grandson, it is true I've told you all the stories in the Scriptures, but the story I tell you now is not like the others. This is the story of everything. What comes next is not what happened to one man or one woman or even to one nation, but it is the cord that ties them all together. You must understand that the Scriptures do not tell many separate stories, but they are one grand narrative that tells the singular, spectacular story of God.

"In the beginning was God. Not the gods of the Greeks or the Romans. Not the Persian gods or the god of any other people, not even of our people. God belongs to no one because no one made Him. He was without beginning and continues without end. God is a being that defies all definition, yet we continue to try to define Him using our simple words and ideas. Today there are gods of every kind. People have made gods of love and pleasure, gods of war and death, and gods of every other thing they can imagine. These are not true gods. They are ideas brought into existence by the imagination of people. If they are gods, then people are the true gods because humans have made these images and idols.

"No, the God of which I speak is the God that did not come from someone's imagination, but the God that made us and gave us imagination. The one true God who made the stars to shine in the heavens and the earth upon which we live. God is not like us. We, in fact, are like Him. The Scriptures tell us that He made us in His own image. In the same way that you reflect the image of your father, God designed us to reflect His image.

"Maybe this is why people today believe they are gods. We see in ourselves the reflection of God and believe that reflection to be the real thing. Do not be deceived by a reflection.

When you see your image in a basin of water, you know that to be only a reflection. You are not in the basin, only water is there. You are so much more than the reflection itself. Likewise, God is so much more than you or I. Though God made us to reflect Him, we are not Him. Anything that is fashioned by humans, no matter how lovely or good, can never be God."

At this the old woman paused. She studied the face of her grandson. She could tell his mind was racing, but he offered no comment or question. She allowed the silence to speak for another moment, then began anew. "There is so much we don't understand about God, but what we do know about God comes from what He has made. I've taught you how God created all that exists in just six days."

"And how on the seventh day He rested, as should your grandson!" interjected Eunice from across the room. Timothy squirmed in his spot and shot his mother a look. Lois continued unabated.

"Yes, and on the seventh day He rested. Look at all He created. The light, the seas and the heaven, the land and the plants, the sun and the moon, the birds and the fish, the animals, and finally humans were all created because God desired to display both His power and His goodness. What good is it to be God with infinite power if you never do anything with it? So, God created a spectacular universe, filled with all kinds of wonder and mystery to display the extent of His great power. Yet, power alone was not all He had to display. God chose to reveal Himself in an intimate, personal manner, so He created humans. Adam came first, but because God loved Adam, He also made Eve, to be Adam's companion. He gave them authority to rule over the land.

"And what a land that was! God's creation was flawless. He brought everything into existence only by speaking. And He spoke only good. No mistakes marred the earth. No evil, sin, death, or sickness existed. God had created a paradise where Adam and Eve could not only live but thrive. There was no need for them to work. If Adam or Eve was hungry, they simply reached out to take fruit from a tree to eat. God had provided for everything.

"The greatest part of creation, though, was not creation itself, but the family that resulted from it. You see, my dear Timothy, God invited Adam and Eve to join in fellowship with Him. While they were merely the creation, God now offered them friendship. All the power, love, and goodness that God displayed in creation were now available for their benefit. Adam and Eve walked with God in the garden. They knew God. They saw His power, knew His love, and benefited from His goodness."

"Now, Timothy, what is it that we must know about God when we examine the creation story?" Lois asked her grandson.

Timothy looked at his grandmother, then toward the door. He knew his friends would leave soon. He glanced at his mother who was now washing a pot. "She didn't ask me. I'm not going to help you," was the response written on his mother's tight-lipped face. Timothy looked back to his grandmother.

"It's not a story about Adam, but about God. God is the one who has power, not people," replied Timothy. His grandmother's piercing eyes were waiting for more. Timothy ventured a guess, "Because God made us in His image, we are supposed to be a reflection of Him?"

"You don't seem so sure about that. Why do you hesitate?" asked Lois.

Timothy thought of all that his grandmother had just said. Then he thought of all the hardships his family had endured in the last year. Timothy could hold his peace no longer. "If God made everything so good, why is there so much bad? If we're supposed to reflect God, why are there so many people that reflect nothing good? If God didn't make sickness or death, why were you so sick last year? Why did my father have to die?" The last words of Timothy's outburst hung in the air. On the other side of the room, Eunice froze, the half-washed pot still in her hands.

In the silence Lois never took her eyes from her grandson's, yet in her heart and in her mind, she was praying for wisdom and words. Finally, with a smile, she replied, "I thought this was a talk about you going out with your friends."

"My friends will wait, or they can go without me. Please, help me to understand."

"For that, we'll need to continue the story."

Chapter 2

The Choice

Timothy shifted where he sat, but couldn't bring himself to look at his grandmother. The hurt that he had been holding inside for so long had just exploded all over the room. More than a year had passed since his father had died, but try as he might, there was only pain and sadness when he thought of him. He had tried to be strong for his mother and his grandmother. His mother had cried for a week after his death. Then one night, she cleaned the house in the middle of the night and began going about her life again. He knew she was trying to be strong, but he still heard her crying sometimes at night.

His grandmother had become ill shortly after the funeral. Many nights had passed with Timothy and his mother sitting by her bedside, nursing her the best they could. Timothy had been afraid that she would follow his father into the grave, but after the physician from Iconium came two months ago, she had begun to feel better. The treatment had worked. While the sickness had left her weak, she appeared to be out of danger now. It hadn't seemed fair to share his pain when he knew they were hurting as well. But now, it was no longer a secret. He had said it. He had told them how unfair it all seemed. In his head he knew that God had created everything and that His creation was good. But in his heart, Timothy wondered how

God could take his father, why God allowed his grandmother such sickness. He knew he should be happy she was still alive, and he was happy she was still here, but the questions remained. Maybe she did have the answers.

"Now, Timothy, you know the story of creation and what came next. Tell me what happened with Adam and Eve in the garden," Lois asked in a gentle, loving voice.

Timothy looked up. There were tears in his grandmother's eyes. Maybe there were tears in his eyes too. "God gave Adam and Eve a rule He knew they couldn't follow. The wicked one tempted Eve to break the rule and Adam and Eve ate the forbidden fruit. Then God cursed them and sent them out of the garden."

"Yes, those things happened, but there's so much more to the story. God gave Adam and Eve all they needed to succeed. He did this because He loved them. But love like that was not enough. Love is a wind that blows both ways. You know that your mother and I love you because since you were born, we have provided for, helped with, and taught you all that you have needed. We have given so that you might have. Likewise, I know you love me because you never left my side while I was sick. You cared for me and that care showed your love. God displayed His love for Adam and Eve by supplying everything they needed. Yet, there was no way for them to show their love for God. They could not give something to God that God had not first created Himself. God needs nothing, so there was nothing Adam and Eve could give.

"So, to allow them a way to show their love and to express their gratitude, God gave a law, just a single rule. With this rule came the choice to obey or disobey God. Obedience to Him would show love and gratitude, disobedience would be a rejection of God. Adam and Eve faced this choice together. Their actions would show the desire of their hearts. The rule God gave them was simple, merely a matter of restraint. God told Adam and Eve not to eat from a specific tree in the garden, the tree of the knowledge of good and evil. To refrain from eating would show their trust in God. Obedience would demonstrate their love and gratitude to Him. They would convey to God the love He desired. Their action would say that they were satisfied with only the knowledge of good that God had already shown them. However, to eat of the fruit would show their lack of trust in God. Disobedience would be a rejection not only of God, but of all that He had done for humanity. It would say that God's goodness was not enough, that they desired the knowledge of evil also."

Eunice had finished her work for the moment and came and sat next to her son. "And just like a good parent," Eunice said to Timothy, "God wanted Adam and Eve to choose what was good. He wanted them to obey. Timothy, I want the same for you too. I want you to know the goodness of God. You must understand that the possibility of evil only existed because love demands a choice. But the path of evil drew Adam and Eve like a flame draws a moth. Only death results from such a choice."

"Your mother is right, Timothy. Of course, she's exactly like her mother." They all smiled then Lois continued, "All God desired from Adam and Eve was their trust and the obedience that results from such trust. This would demonstrate their love toward God. But Adam and Eve together chose to disobey God's rule. Their actions were the answer that spoke to their lack of faith in God. Their disobedience was the key that unlocked the door to sin and death. God did not bring those things into the world, humans did. Sin and death, and disease along with them, are humanity's gift to the world because we chose the knowledge of evil.

"Adam and Eve tried to cover their shame by using leaves to make clothes. Because of their guilt and fear, they hid when

God came to find them. The knowledge of good and evil had shown them their mistake and they were embarrassed, ashamed. But this was not the end of Adam, nor of the story of God. God reached out to Adam. In His infinite wisdom, God prepared a way to redeem humanity. First, though, there must be consequences for their actions. The consequences would serve to remind Adam and Eve of the choice they had made. The serpent, who tempted them to disobey, was cursed to be feared by humans and to crawl on the ground. Woman would have pain in childbirth and be subject to her husband. Man would have to labor to provide food for him and his family. Then God took the life of a lamb, first as a reminder to them that sin results in death, then to clothe and cover the shame of His fallen creation."

"Couldn't God have found some other way that they could have shown their love?" Timothy questioned. "Some way that wouldn't end with death?"

"But, Timothy, death isn't the end. Yes, everyone dies. Some leave this world because of illness, others because of war. Some die after they have lived a long life, others leave us far too soon. Death separates us from those we love," Lois said, then paused as the loss of her son-in-law lingered in their minds. "But death is only the end of this life. The Scriptures tell us that God will give life to the dead. The one who created us will give life to His people in the world to come. Death brings sadness to those left behind, but it is nothing we should fear. Eunice, how does that song go? The one you were singing earlier."

Eunice drew her breath, then in a low, soft voice sang, "Even though I walk through the valley of the shadow of death, I will fear no evil: for You are with me." Timothy's mother had sung that song to him since before he could remember. Now the words came flooding into his mind as she sang it again. When she finished the song, Timothy turned back to his grandmother."

"No, what we should fear is not death. We should fear making the wrong choice. Just like Adam and Eve, each of us face the same choice. Do I trust God? We see the consequences of answering no, but we must see the reward for choosing yes. Sin's choice led to death, but choosing to trust God leads to the restoration of our soul. He who trusts in God will find peace in His protection and provision. Goodness and mercy are the reward of those who dwell in the house of God. God does not promise to remove us from the consequences of sin, but when we choose Him, He will be with us as we pass through them. Right now, we are still living in the shadow of your father's death. But God has not abandoned us here, He is leading us past this dark valley to a place where we can see His goodness.

"God's desire is, and always has been, to redeem and restore fallen humanity. That's how much He loves us. That's why He promised Adam and Eve that, while sin would cause us to stumble, He would send someone to triumph over sin. When the Messiah comes, He will free us from the power of sin and death and will restore us back to the family of God. Your father died because death is the consequence of sin. God did not bring death, but God will do away with it. The resurrection and the promise to defeat sin and death are the actions of a loving God. He asks only for our love in return. Our actions are the answer to the question He asks, 'Do you trust God?'"

Timothy stood up. He crossed the room toward the window. Lois looked at her daughter, then reached out her hand. Eunice took her hand and squeezed it tight. Timothy was not the only one that needed healing. As Timothy stood looking out the window, Lois could hear him humming softly. Eunice stood and went back to the kitchen to place the bread in the oven and to finish preparations for the Sabbath. Sunset would arrive in only two more hours and she needed to finish many things before then. As she added wood to the fire, Eunice heard the door open. Before either woman could ask Timothy where he was going, he was gone.

Chapter 3

Consequence

Timothy just walked. At first he had no direction in mind, he just needed to be alone. His mind raced as he walked through the dusty streets of Lystra. As he reached the main gate of the city, he thought of all his grandmother had said. It was true, he feared death. It seemed as if death had been too close to his family for far too long. Timothy continued past the Temple of Zeus and then raced down the hill out of the city proper. Only when he reached the shade of a juniper tree did he stop. As he sat down under the tree, he looked back. From here he could see the entire village. In truth, there wasn't much to see, just a collection of homes sitting on top of a small hill. Only the temple to the Greek god was of any note. There were beggars and cripples outside its doors. The same ones had been there for years on end, waiting for their gods to help them. In the center of the village was a large open plaza where merchants sold their goods. It was there that his friends were waiting for him. He should be there now, laughing with them. But here he was, trying to figure out the answer to his grandmother's question, "Do you trust God?"

None of his friends were Jews. He couldn't ask them about this. They would never understand his Jewish heritage. Only one other Jewish boy lived in Lystra, but he was younger than

Timothy. He wouldn't understand either. The only other Jewish boys he knew were the ones he had met at the synagogue in Iconium. His mother had taken him every chance she could when he was little, but that was before his father died. Then his grandmother had been sick. Maybe now that she felt better they would begin to attend synagogue again. Perhaps that would calm his conscience. No, this was not something that would wait. Why did growing up have to be so difficult? Life had been so much simpler when he was younger. Timothy watched the clouds as they floated over his home. Soon the sun would set. He should return home. His mother was sure to be worried. Timothy rose and headed back home. He stopped along the path to pick some wildflowers. Maybe the flowers would be an acceptable apology for running out so suddenly.

*

Eunice stared out the window, as if her stare could somehow make her son come home. While the bread was baking, she had finished preparations to welcome the Sabbath. Everything was in its place. The meals were finished, there was sufficient water for the next day, the table was set, and she had cleaned all that she could. Only the bread remained in the oven. Her husband had once said that the hot bread was his favorite part of welcoming the Sabbath. She had always left it to finish just before sundown because of this. Even though he was no longer here, the ritual remained.

Where is my son? prayed Eunice. *Please God, help him to understand. Show him Your way. Bring him home tonight.*

Before she completed her prayer, the door swung open and Timothy entered. In his hands was a large bouquet of wildflowers. "I'm sorry, *Immah*," was all he could say before Eunice had wrapped him in a warm embrace.

"It's okay. I miss him too," she replied, pushing back the tears.

Timothy handed her the flowers, "I thought these would look nice for the Sabbath."

"They're wonderful. Now go clean up, it'll be sunset soon."

Eunice placed the flowers in a vase on the table then turned to remove the bread from the oven. Timothy washed his hands and face in the basin then went to the back room to change his clothes. A few moments later he returned and set two candles on the table. Lois and Eunice moved to the table and each lit a candle, repeating a short blessing to welcome the Sabbath. Together they sat down to eat, three generations of family, united again in this moment.

The three ate in silence until Timothy spoke, this time in a gentler voice that sought answers, not argument, "It doesn't seem fair. The consequences of Adam and Eve's sin. Why should something that happened so long ago have any impact on my life today? If a person steals, he should pay the price, not his descendants thousands of years later. How does that make sense?"

Timothy looked to his grandmother. Lois reached for the bread and took another piece. "You're correct. It would be unfair for someone thousands of years removed from the crime to pay the price. But that's not really what is happening, is it? Adam and Eve made their choice and as a result sin and death became a part of the world. This is no different from the impact that your parents marrying and moving to Lystra had on you. They did not consult you for your opinion on these matters as you had yet to be born. However, their decision has had a profound impact on your life. Instead of being a child of only one people, you are equally part of two different peoples. Instead of growing up surrounded by Jewish friends in Israel, you've grown up surrounded by Greek friends here. Part of your identity will always be defined by things out of your control, they're just part of your heritage, part of your nature. You're from Lystra. You're both Jew and Greek, for better or for worse. Besides, it's not entirely fair to judge Adam and Eve for their actions. How many of us would have done any differently than them?" Lois paused as she pushed her plate away.

"I think it's time we reexamined the story of the first family. After God sent Adam and Eve out of the garden, they began their family. God gifted them with two wonderful sons, Cain and Abel. I imagine Adam and Eve were thrilled. God had sent them not one, but two sons. Perhaps they thought that one of them would be the one to defeat sin. Cain was skilled in the labor of the fields and Abel was skilled in the care of the flocks. Just like their parents, the sons of Adam faced the same choice whether they would trust God or not. Yet, just like their parents, they were willful and sinned against God. But we know that Adam taught his sons about the sacrifice God made for their sin, because the Scriptures tell us that both the sons of Adam brought sacrifices to God. There would have been no need for them to offer such a sacrifice if they were without sin. Neither Cain nor Abel would be the one to defeat sin.

"Cain's pride led him to bring a sacrifice of his finest harvest. Abel humbly brought the firstborn lamb. Cain's offering did not please God because it was an offering of his own effort and it failed to recognize the consequence of sin. But God accepted Abel's offering because it was the lamb who paid the price. The death of the lamb showed that Abel understood the consequence of sin. Cain's sacrifice showed that he still did not trust God, but Abel's sacrifice showed that he had learned to trust Him. Anger filled Cain because God accepted his brother's sacrifice but rejected his. This anger led Cain to choose the path of sin and it was on that path that he killed his brother. Sin always leads to death.

"All of Adam's children, from that day until this, have been guilty of sin. Not only because Adam and Eve sinned, but because each of us, in our own way, have chosen to not trust God. Sometimes it seems as simple as telling an untruth or breaking the Sabbath. Other times it appears more grievous in our eyes, such as causing harm to someone or even killing someone. But each of these actions, small and large, shows that we, as humans, have chosen our own way–not trusting God."

"But what of those that are like Abel and choose to trust God and obey Him?" questioned Timothy. "They still die, don't they?"

"Yes, Timothy, they still die. God forgives those who turn to Him, but the consequence of sin still remains. Death will be part of our world as long as sin is. Only God can completely defeat sin and death. He has promised that He will. He will send one who is not under the judgement of sin. The Messiah will make a way for us all to be free from sin and death."

"You said that I'm both Jew and Greek, but these are both sons of Adam," Timothy began to explain. "Sin exists because of him, but each of us is equally responsible for the wrong choice we have made. We've all made the same wrong choice Adam did. So, we all deserve the same consequence of sin—death."

"Yes, Timothy, that's correct," replied Lois. "Whether we admit it or not, the consequence of sin is fair. God is just. He offered a better way, but we rejected it. All we can do now is admit our guilt and seek after God." The three of them sat in silence for a moment. They had finished eating long ago. Looking at each other, they repeated a prayer of thanksgiving.

Eunice stood first. "It's getting late. I'm going to bed. Timothy, I'm proud of the man you are becoming. I love you."

"I love you too, *Immah*. Goodnight." Timothy kissed his mother on the cheek.

"Timothy, before you go, would you move my chair over by the window?" asked Lois. "I want to look at the stars tonight." Timothy moved her chair over by the window and tied the curtain back. Then he helped his grandmother to her chair. As she sat down, she grabbed Timothy's arm and pulled him close. She whispered something in his ear, then prayed, "O God in Heaven, teach my grandson to trust you. As I have learned to trust you, may he learn even more so."

Timothy pulled back and looked at his grandmother. She loved him more than anyone, of that he was sure. He placed the blanket once more on her lap, then kissed her cheek and said good night. Timothy went to his bed. As he lay down, his grandmother's prayer and the words she had whispered raced through his mind. *Trust in the Lord with all your heart and lean not on your own understanding.*

That's what trust is, believing what you can't understand, thought Timothy. *Why does it have to be so hard?* Timothy turned in his bed. *Hopefully, sleep will come easier than trust.*

Chapter 4

Redemption

The sun had not yet begun to peek over the horizon when Timothy decided that sleep was no longer worth chasing. He rolled out of bed more tired than he had been the night before. Careful not to wake his mother, he headed for the door. If he couldn't sleep, at least he could watch the sun rise. He carefully opened the door and pulled it shut behind him. The air was cool. Timothy took a few deep breaths then walked to the side of the house to watch the sunrise.

"You couldn't sleep either?" Timothy jumped. The voice of his grandmother startled him. Lois rested on a large rock facing the horizon, wrapped in her blanket. Without turning, she called, "Come sit next to me. We can watch the sunrise together." Timothy looked at the old woman. In the darkness she appeared more silhouette than substance. As he sat down next to her, though, he reassured himself that she was more than just a dream. The soft rasp of her breathing and the warmth of her body assured him that she was there, just as he was.

They sat in the cool of the morning for a few minutes waiting for the first signs of light. Lois spoke, "You know, God could have abandoned us. Could have left us to our own devices after we had shown that we cared little for God and less for our brother. In fact, there are those who believe that's precisely what God did. They believe that God created everything, set it in motion, and then just stepped back to watch the results. And for a time, it does seem to be what happened, although I believe God was simply waiting to give us time to choose Him. Regardless, after Cain killed his brother many hundreds of years passed before God spoke again. There were some who followed their own paths for a brief time, then learned to follow the path of faith, but most continued down the path of self toward their own destruction. Even those who chose to trust God were unable to stem the tide of evil that came."

"You're talking about the flood," Timothy responded. "God sent the flood to destroy the world. Only Noah and his family escaped death."

"Yes, I'm talking about the flood. But not the flood you're thinking about. Noah's flood came second. The first flood was the evil that covered the land because of humanity's choice to pursue their own will instead of trusting God. Yes, Noah's flood came second. But the story of the flood is so much more than destruction and death. It's a story about the consequences of sin and God's plan of redemption."

"Redemption?" asked Timothy. "How is this story about redemption?"

"God looked down at the world and saw that people did only that which pleased themselves," Lois continued. "The perfect world He had created for us was in ruin. No one thought about God. Except for Noah. Noah chose to trust God and walked the path of faith, just as Abel had in the beginning. God told Noah of the coming destruction and commanded him to build an ark, a boat that would serve to protect both human and animal life in the coming flood. You see, God sent the flood not simply to destroy those that had chosen their own path, but to cleanse the world of the evil that had consumed it. God grieved that He made us, not because humans were an awful creation, but because they had chosen to reject Him and had brought evil upon the entire land.

"So, just as a potter who destroys his flawed creation to make a new one, God decided to make a fresh start. He would redeem, reclaim this fallen creation. This would not be like the first time, however. The first time, He had created from nothing, using only the power of His words. This time, He would use the existing world, but first He would cleanse the land. The flood cleansed and remade the earth in a new form. Then, instead of creating a new man as He had done with Adam, He took one, Noah, who had already learned the lesson of trusting God. But Noah did not enter the ark alone. Noah's family, his wife and three sons along with their wives, joined him in trusting God. Even more, Noah preached the message of faith to all who would hear him. God offered His invitation of redemption to all, but only Noah and his family responded. The day came when God sent the animals, two by two, male and female, aboard the ark. The eight members of Noah's family also entered. The door closed, then God sent the waters both to destroy and to cleanse. God destroyed all the evil that people had done, and He cleansed the earth for a new beginning.

"Noah was not better than other people, but his choice was. He chose to trust God and that faith moved him to obey. He did as God commanded and built the ark. He preached righteousness so that people would know of their sin and repent of it. Sin's guarantee is that death comes to all people. Noah simply told them of the day and the way death would come, but they all rejected Noah's message and the salvation God offered. All they had to do was trust God and they could have boarded the ark as well. None did.

"For a year, the ark sat upon the waters. When God dried the land and Noah and his family left the ark, everything was different. All who entered the ark had been redeemed unto a new land. God desires to redeem all people, to make all things right. The only way through the flood was on the ark and the only way to be made right with God is to trust Him. Salvation is of the Lord. God knew that evil still existed in our hearts, but he promised Noah that he would never destroy the earth again as He had just done. The need for redemption will arise again, but it will come in another way. The rainbow in the sky reminds us of that promise and the hope we have that God will redeem us again."

The two sat in silence as now the sun appeared. First, a glimmer of light emerged off the horizon, then streaks of red and orange shone as the sun rose higher. Suddenly, the reds and oranges disappeared as the bright yellow and white light of the sun raced across the sky. The dark of night faded as the bright blue of the morning sky appeared overhead. Timothy wrapped an arm around his grandmother and squeezed her tight.

"A person could be jealous watching the two of you out here."

Timothy turned. "*Immah*! Good morning. I didn't want to wake you," he exclaimed as he rose to kiss her cheek.

"And I thank you for that. I only woke in time to catch the end of the sunrise. How long have you two been out here?" asked Eunice.

"Long enough for Noah to build his ark and for God to reclaim His fallen creation," Timothy responded with a smile. "Did you realize that God wasn't just destroying the world, but was giving us a second chance to choose to trust Him?"

"Is that so?" replied Eunice. She looked to her mother then back to Timothy. "Why do you think He did that?"

"Well," Timothy paused. "I think sin makes God as sad as it does us. He wants us to choose Him just as He chose us. That's why He waited so long after Adam to send the flood, He wanted people to choose good, but they only chose evil. I think our hearts are broken. Why else would we continually choose wrong?"

"You're right, Timothy. Our hearts are broken, and that breaks God's heart." Eunice hugged her son. "And that's why God promised to send the Messiah. To fix our broken hearts and to be the Redeemer that will conquer death and sin once for all."

Lois sat, fixated on the sun, soaking in its warmth as it rose into the sky. Still facing the sun, she began to sing,

O my God, I cry in the daytime, but You do not answer;
and at night, but I have no rest.
But You are holy,
O You who inhabits the praises of Israel.
Our fathers trusted in You;
they trusted, and You did deliver them.
They cried to You and were delivered;
they trusted in You and were not put to shame.

Timothy listened to the words. *At night I have no rest. That's me*, he thought. Suddenly, he was tired. Why did it feel like he was chasing something he couldn't catch? Timothy turned to go back inside. Eunice went to help her mother to her feet. Arm in arm the two women moved back into the house. Eunice helped her mother to her chair then turned to find Timothy. At first, she didn't see him, but then she noticed the door to the back room was open. She looked inside. Her son was asleep in his bed.

Chapter 5

The Promise

The house was not large, nor was it fancy, but it was home. Eunice looked around. The house had been built by her husband and his father when her husband was only a boy. There were just two rooms, the large central room and a small bedroom in the back. The fireplace was in the middle on the far wall of the large room. The bread oven in the corner of the fireplace was an addition her husband had built specially for her. A window faced the street in the front and the entrance opened on a small courtyard to the side. Bed mattresses for her and her mother lay in the corner right next to the fireplace. A small table, where the family ate, stood in the front part of the room. The small room in the back was Timothy's. It contained only a mattress, a large closet, and a small window. She had shared that room with her husband, but could no longer sleep there, not for more than a year now. When Timothy asked if he could, she had granted his request. She had convinced herself it was because Timothy needed a bit of privacy now that he was becoming a man, not because of her own reluctance to enter.

She pictured her husband's face. He had loved telling the story of how he built the house, mixing the mortar, carrying bricks. In truth his father had done most of the work, but the way her husband told the story, he had built this palace all on his own. Each brick told a story. That's why she loved him so much. There was always a story. Stories brought laughter and joy. But also, maybe, that's why he had loved her. Even though they came from different worlds, the stories she had told him of her God and her faith in Him had convinced him to share her God and her faith.

She shared her faith with him and then he shared his homeland with her. They had married back in Caesarea but moved to Lystra shortly thereafter. The death of her father had been difficult, but she was glad when her mother had come to live with them in Lystra. Timothy was born soon after that and the entire family had rejoiced in the birth of a son. Timothy had grown so fast. She remembered when he took his first steps. Just on the other side of the room he had walked to his grandfather. Only three steps, but her father-in-law had declared them to be the grandest steps any person had ever taken. He proclaimed a feast that day in the name of Zeus. She frowned. Her in-laws had never accepted the truth of the God of heaven and died believing in their Greek gods. Her husband had tried to convince them, but they had refused. Before Timothy was two, they had both passed. For many years it had been only the four of them, Eunice and her husband, Lois, and Timothy. Now, only three remained.

It was nearly midday when Timothy awoke. He came sheepishly into the room. "God rested on the seventh day and so does my grandson," Lois smiled. "Don't worry, though, we would have woken you if it was time to eat."

"Thank you for that. Although if you had waited any longer to wake me, it appears I may have gone hungry," replied Timothy looking at the table with the food already set out. In the center of the table was a small roasted pheasant that he had trapped last week. Next to it was a large *challah*, the delicious braided bread that his mother made. Olives, dried figs, and nuts completed the setting. "I'll be right back." Timothy was gone for just a moment, then returned inside to wash his hands in the basin. Timothy knelt next to his mother and grandmother as they recited a portion of the *Torah* then prayed. Together they sang a psalm of praise, then gathered around the table to begin their meal.

"Timothy, what can you tell me about our father Abraham?" Eunice asked.

"He was a righteous man that God made into a great people, our people. The Jews. He had two sons, one the son of a slave, Ishmael, and the other the son of promise, Isaac. From Isaac came Jacob who wrestled with God. God changed his name to Israel and from him came the twelve tribes of our people."

"Very good. Now why is any of this important to us today?" Eunice asked.

"It's important because..." Timothy paused. "It's important because...I don't know. Because we should know the history of our people?"

"Yes, we should know our history. Knowing our history helps to guide our future," Eunice answered. "So, tell me, my son, who are our people?"

"We are the children of Israel, the chosen of God," Timothy quickly replied. This answer he knew, or at least he thought he did. The look his mother was giving him made him rethink his answer.

"We are the children of Israel," Eunice confirmed, "and of his father, Isaac, and of his father, Abraham. And it is true that God chose our people. But there is so much more to the story. And it's certainly not a story about just one man and his family. It's a story about everyone and the God who made us. It's the story of promise." Eunice stopped for a moment. Her mother had been telling this story to Timothy. Maybe she should let her continue the story. She looked to her mother, who was watching her in anticipation. *No, this is my story to tell*, she thought.

"The story of Abram is the story of promise. Not just a promise made to Abram, but the promise made to Adam and Eve that God would defeat sin and death. God had not forgotten His promise made so long ago. Adam and Eve had died, but their descendants lived on. Many chose their own way and allowed evil to fill the earth, but God cleansed the earth. He began new with Noah. But exactly like the first time, people chose their own way and failed to trust God. Our pride led only to sin. God promised Noah that He would not destroy the earth again, so now He did something different. He chose a single man. When God chose Noah to build an ark, it was because Noah walked the path of faith. Not this time. This time He chose a man, just an ordinary man. God promised this man that He would make from him a great people. God would make his name great on the earth. God would bless those who blessed him and curse those who cursed him.

"Some might hear this and say that God was playing favorites, but that's not the case. Lost in all of this is the reason God promised Abram all these things. Twice in the promise God tells Abram that He is doing this so that Abram will be a blessing. In Abram's family, all the world would be blessed. God's favor was not so Abram would become fat and wealthy. It was not permission for our people to do whatever we pleased. It was a mission. God's mission: To fulfill His promise to Adam and Eve and defeat sin and death. And He selected Abram to be the one whose family would demonstrate God's favor on earth. God would bless Israel and the world would be drawn to the God of Israel. The world would learn to trust God.

"But first, Abram had to learn to trust God. God told Abram to leave his home and go to a place God would show him. In his first step of faith, Abram obeyed. He left his home and began the journey that would last the rest of his life. The story of Abram is long and far from perfect, but the part we must understand is the promise. God's promise came true in that Abram gained a great name and great wealth, but Abram was troubled by the fact that he had no heir. How could the promise of a great nation come from a man with no son? Abram believed God's word to be true but wanted to understand. He asked God if his servant Eliezer was to be his heir. God told him that he would have a son born of his own seed.

"Sometimes the road of faith leads to places where we cannot see the path ahead. We stumble in the dark over unseen obstacles. We fall down. But in that moment, we must learn to call out to God for help. When the road is dark and fear surrounds us, in that moment we must learn to trust God. For Abram, this was one of those times. Abram trusted God and it was his faith that made him right with God. Yet, he tried his own way to provide an heir. He could not see the road ahead and he tried to forge his own way. His wife sent her servant to Abram and he had a child with her."

"Hagar and Ishmael," said Timothy quietly.

"Yes, Ishmael. The boy was Abram's joy. And God made him a great people because of Abram. Ishmael was not a mistake, but neither was he the promised son. God changed the names of Abram and Sarai and promised Abraham a son born to Sarah in her old age. God promised to provide a child to them even after nature said that it was too late. Isaac, the son God promised, was born. I remember the joy your father had when you were born. He walked on clouds for weeks just because he had a son. Timothy, he loved you so much." Eunice paused to wipe away a tear. "I imagine for Abraham it must have been the same. His miracle son was born. But Isaac was more than just a son to Abraham, he was the fulfillment of the promise God had made. The promise of a great nation and a blessing to all people was not just a hope but was made real in the birth of Isaac. Abraham would teach his son to trust God just as he had learned to do. Abraham looked at the night sky and knew that in Isaac his family would be more numerous than the stars in heaven, just as God had promised."

"And just like the stars in heaven, God wants us to be a light, a light pointing people to the one true God," Timothy exclaimed. "That all makes sense. God knew that people would choose their own way if He didn't do something to help them understand. That's why He wants us to obey. Our obedience shows our faith and our faith is what the world needs to see."

"I couldn't have said it better myself," Lois added. "Abraham trusted God. That is what each person, from the family of Israel or not, must do. God set Abraham as a light to draw the world to Him. By trusting God in obedience to His commands, we show the world that God can be trusted and encourage them to come to God. Timothy, too many of our own people have forgotten that God is not the God of Israel alone, but of all people. Never forget that. God wants all people to trust him."

"Like *Papà*," said Timothy. "He followed the God of heaven and not the Greek gods."

"Like your father. Your mother told him about the true God, and he chose to trust Him," replied Lois. Then with a quick smile, added, "And then he married your mother and gave me the greatest gift I have ever received, a grandson."

Timothy blushed with pride, then his thoughts turned to what he had heard. God is not only the God of the Jews, but of the Greeks and the Romans and of all the other peoples too. He liked that thought. A God for all people, one that anyone can trust.

Chapter 6

Trust

As Timothy rested his head back against the cushions, he smiled. For the first time in his young life, God was beginning to make sense. Always before the rules and traditions of his mother and grandmother's religion had seemed like ropes tying him down and holding him back. Now the ropes loosened and fell away to reveal a God who loved people and wanted their love in return. God did not desire obedience as much as the trust that obedience signified.

Timothy looked around the room. They had finished their meal and moved closer to the fireplace. There was no fire in it. The weather was not yet cold enough to need one other than for cooking. Besides, today was the Sabbath and there would be no cooking. His grandmother was in her chair, her eyes closed. Timothy could not decide if she was sleeping or just resting her eyes. His mother sat beside him on the floor, leaning against one of the cushions. Four large cushions were piled on the floor and arranged in a semicircle. His mother and grandmother had made them two summers ago along with new bed mattresses for the whole family. Father had made a deal with a cloth merchant and traded for a whole bolt of fabric. The women had worked the fabric while he had helped father collect the reeds and straw to fill them. They had made several trips out into the fields to collect the materials. It was hot work, but it was worth it. He remembered feeling like a king sleeping on the new mattress that night. Timothy looked at the pillows, then over to the corner where two bed mattresses lay. They all needed new stuffing. He would start collecting straw and reeds this week. They would need to dry before he could change the filling, but he needed to do it. His mother and grandmother would certainly appreciate it as well. Mother had helped him last year to collect the straw, but Timothy was sure he could do it alone this year.

He looked back to his mother and asked, "What happened next? You said that Abraham learned to trust God, what about Isaac? How did he learn to trust God?"

Eunice looked at her son. *He's hungry, looking for the truth. Instead of looking at the stories from the Scriptures as just stories, he's beginning to see how they all fit together. He's learning to trust God.* "Of course, Isaac didn't remain a child. He grew, just as you have," Eunice explained. "Abraham knew that God would fulfill His promise in Isaac. Yet, the day came that God asked a very strange thing from Abraham."

"He asked Abraham to sacrifice Isaac," Timothy interjected.

"Yes, God asked Abraham to sacrifice the son of promise," Eunice answered. "The one in whom He had already stated that the promise would be fulfilled. This was a strange request in several ways. First, we know that God values human life. A human sacrifice has never been acceptable to God. Human life is what God desires to redeem. People offer an animal sacrifice in the place of their sin, not the life of another person. Second, even accepting that Abraham would offer Isaac as a human sacrifice, if Isaac died, God's promise would be broken. How could God ask Abraham to do this? If God's promise was broken, then people could no longer trust God. We would remain without hope. Sin and death would be permanent residents of this earth.

"Abraham took his son and two servants on a journey. Three days they traveled. I wonder when Isaac noticed there was no animal for the sacrifice. Maybe it was right away. Perhaps he thought they would stop and take one from their herds or buy one from a shepherd along the way. Either way, I'm sure he never guessed that he was the intended sacrifice. Abraham didn't tell him either. I wonder if Abraham ever reconsidered. If God wanted a human sacrifice, Abraham could have offered one of the servants, not his beloved son. But no, God had asked for Isaac by name. He would give his son as a sacrifice to God because he trusted God. God must have some other plan. Either He would stop him from killing his son, or God would bring him back from the dead, but Abraham was determined to obey God regardless of the task."

"Do you really think he would have killed Isaac?" Timothy asked. "Would you have done it?"

The question stopped Eunice in her story. It was one thing for Abraham to give his son, but for her to give Timothy…. "I hope God never asks such a thing from me, but I pray that I might trust God as Abraham did." She looked deeply into her son's eyes. He was looking back just the same. "God never breaks His word. I trust Him, with my life and yours." Timothy held her gaze for a moment, then looked away. Eunice waited to see if he had another question, but he said nothing, so she continued. "Abraham left the servants at the base of the mountain and told them that both he and the boy would return. He trusted God with what would happen. As they climbed the mountain, Isaac finally asked his father where the sacrifice was. Abraham replied that God would provide the sacrifice. You know the rest, they reach the top, Isaac was bound and placed on the altar. Abraham lifted his knife to slay his son, but the angel of the Lord stopped him. God showed Abraham a ram caught in a bush and they offered it in Isaac's place. Through the whole ordeal, Abraham never showed that he doubted God. He obeyed, convinced that God would not take the son He had promised."

"Why did God go to such lengths to test Abraham?" questioned Timothy. "Did God not know the depths of Abraham's faith?"

"Oh, no," Eunice answered. "God didn't do this to test Abraham. Of course, God knew how much Abraham trusted Him. He asked Abraham to do this so that the world would know how much he trusted God. Remember, God's favor on Abraham was so that he would be a blessing to others, so that all the nations would know God. God did this, asking Abraham for the son of promise, so that everyone would see what faith looks like. God set Abraham and Isaac on a mountain so that all the world could see a man that trusts God. We must follow the example of Abraham. If God asks for your entire world, as Isaac was to Abraham, then we must trust that God will provide a new world. God knows our hearts, but we must learn to know the heart of God.

"But also, the lesson was for Isaac. God would make the same promise to Isaac and to his son Jacob that He had made to Abraham. Each in turn had to learn to trust God themselves. I believe that in the moment when God stopped the knife, Isaac learned to trust God. He saw that his father trusted God with his life and God was faithful to save him. He learned to trust God himself."

Eunice looked out the window. Soon the sun would set, and the Sabbath would be over. "Timothy, the promise of God to Abraham, Isaac, and Jacob is the same promise to you and to me. God's favor is on our people so that we might be a blessing to others. So that we might point the world to God and teach them to trust Him. Yet it is still a choice each man and each woman must make. To live in obedience to God so that the world may see that we trust God and that He is the source of our blessing. Israel is the light that shows the world the way of faith, the way of God."

"*Immah,*" Timothy began, "all my life I have been both Jew and Greek. At home, I'm a Jew, and when I leave home, I'm a Greek. But really, I didn't know who I was. Now I do. Before, I didn't trust God. Now, I am a child of God. I trust God. I trust God like Abel. I trust God like Noah. I trust God like Abraham. I trust God like *Sabta*. I trust God like *Papà*. And I trust God like you. I can do that as a Jew, and I can do that as a Greek, because God wants all people to trust Him. So, I trust Him. But more than that, *Immah*, I think God has put us here so that we can be a light like Abraham. No one else in Lystra knows the true God. But I will trust God and they will all see that the true God is the one that lives in heaven. I can't wait till I can tell my friends."

Eunice hugged her son. "Thank you, God," she whispered in prayer. Long ago she had prayed that this day would come. The day when Timothy would understand what it was to be a Jew. What it was to trust God. Now he not only trusted God, but wanted to be a light to the world, just as God intended. "Help him," she prayed. On the other side of the room, in her chair, Lois smiled as well.

Chapter 7

Outcast

Timothy frowned. It had all made sense when his mother and grandmother explained it. What had he said wrong? Timothy had been full of excitement when he went to meet his friends. Now, as he walked home, Timothy rehearsed in his mind everything that had happened. He had met his friends at the plaza, in their usual place, right before where the merchant stalls begin. Denis, Kirill, Jason, and Darius had all been there. Jason began to tell Timothy a story from the night he had missed. Timothy cut him short. He had news that couldn't wait.

"I need to tell you all about the God that made us," he boldly proclaimed.

"You mean the Titan, right?" Denis interjected. "Everyone knows the Titans made everything including the gods."

"No, I'm talking about what really happened," Timothy responded. "The Titans and gods are all made up tales meant to scare us. I'm talking about the one true God of heaven who made everything including people."

"Are you crazy?" Darius questioned. "You sound like that old spice merchant that comes through here. One God, one God, there's only one God," he sang sarcastically, while doing a mocking imitation of the Jewish merchant. Timothy knew the merchant Darius was mocking and he started to get a bit upset.

"Besides, if your one God really does exist, who made Him? I'll tell you who, Kronos. That's who, because the Titans made the gods and that's what's true."

Timothy kept trying to argue with his friends but the more he argued, the meaner the responses grew. Finally, Kirill shouted, "I thought you were one of us, but you're just a foreign half-breed. Take your Hebrew God back to wherever He came from. Zeus is our god." With that his friends had turned and left without him.

It wasn't supposed to go like that. Timothy only wanted them to understand God in the same way he did. Discouraged and frustrated, he returned home to grab a basket. If his friends wouldn't listen to him, at least he could begin collecting straw for the mattresses and cushions. He rummaged through the old goat stall where he found a large basket, then he turned to fill a waterskin. His grandmother was sitting on the other side of the courtyard watching him.

"What's the matter, Timothy? Why are you upset?" Lois questioned.

"It's nothing," he replied flatly. "I'm going out to the fields to collect straw for the mattresses. Where's the rope for the basket? Never mind, I'll find it."

"It's not nothing, I can tell when my favorite grandson is upset. Tell me what's going on."

Timothy stopped looking for the rope and looked again at his grandmother. "I tried to tell my friends about God. They laughed at me and left without me. I don't understand what I did wrong."

"Oh, Timothy. You didn't do anything wrong," Lois reassured her grandson. "Some people don't want to hear the truth. It takes time for people to adjust the way they think. What do the Scriptures say about this? Do you remember what happened with Joseph and his brothers?"

Timothy leaned against a barrel. "Joseph's brothers hated him and sold him into slavery."

"That's right. And why did they hate him?" Lois asked.

"Because he was their father's favorite. Joseph received the multicolored coat from Israel. Also, he had dreams, dreams where they all bowed down to him," Timothy responded carefully.

"Exactly," Lois answered. "Joseph's brothers were jealous of him because their father favored him and because God had shown him the future. They probably thought that Joseph considered himself better than them. But think about Joseph. He wasn't any better than his brothers. He was just one of the twelve, another one of the sons. It was his father's favor and God's favor that separated him from the others. But the one thing that Joseph did that truly made him special was that he consistently chose to do that which was right. When his brothers did wrong, he did not. He obeyed when his father sent him after his brothers. That's why Israel was able to send Joseph after his brothers, he knew that Joseph would do what was right.

"Israel sent Joseph to find his brothers because he needed someone he could trust. Someone that he knew would do what was right and needed even if he wasn't there to see it. Most people will do what is right when people are watching, but when they are by themselves they give in to wrong. Look at Joseph's brothers. They were good men, but when given the chance to do evil, they did it. Meanwhile, Joseph searched for his brothers from town to town until he found them. He could have given up and returned home, but his father had asked him to find his brothers and to bring a report. So, he followed them until he found them. He obeyed."

"But that obedience cost him everything," Timothy replied. "His brothers almost killed him, then instead, sold him into slavery and told their father he was dead." Timothy could begin to sense where this was going as he thought about his own rejection by his friends.

"Yet, God's plan for Joseph was only beginning," Lois continued. "The dreams God had given him would not be fulfilled unless Joseph went through this painful experience. God used the pain of rejection and the sorrow of loss to shape Joseph into the man he would become. Only God knows what the future holds. His plan is so much greater than ours. Israel sent Joseph after his brothers, but God sent Joseph to Egypt to save his brothers. None of them knew that, but God did. Joseph trusted God and did what was right. So, how about you, Timothy?"

"What do you mean, how about me? Will I go to Egypt and save our family? Sure, I can do that," Timothy offered with a smile. "You mean, 'Do I still trust God if my friends laugh at me and reject me?'"

"Yes, that's what I mean," Lois smiled.

"Yes, I still trust God," Timothy replied. "But why does it have to be so hard? Why wouldn't my friends listen?"

"But they did listen," Lois responded. "They heard everything that you said. They rejected God today, but the day will come when they won't. They will hear your words and God will change their hearts. He will exchange their hearts of stone for hearts of flesh. Don't give up on them. Certainly, don't allow rejection to stop you from doing what faith leads you to do. God allowed Joseph to suffer this persecution to accomplish His plan. You don't know where the road of faith will lead, but you do know He who leads the way. Trust that if you are doing right God will use that. And be ready."

"Ready for what?" Timothy asked.

"Ready for the day when God opens their hearts," Lois answered. "Be ready to speak the words of God to them."

"Okay, *Sabta*. I will," Timothy replied. "But now, I need to get out into the fields. Where is that rope?"

"It's hanging on the post over there," Lois pointed to the rope hanging just behind Timothy.

"Thanks, *Sabta*," Timothy said. "You couldn't have told me that ten minutes ago?"

"And miss this delightful discussion? Not a chance," Lois chuckled. "Don't forget your basket and water."

Timothy grabbed the rope, basket, and waterskin, then headed for the door. As he crossed the entryway toward the front door, his mother called out, "Timothy, take this with you." Eunice stepped out of the house and into the courtyard with a small bundle in her hands. She gave it to him. Timothy could feel the warmth of fresh bread in his hands.

"Thanks, *Immah*. I'll be back as soon as I can." Timothy headed for the city gate. As he walked, he thought about what his grandmother had said. Timothy had been mad at his friends when they rejected his ideas about God. They had laughed at him and called him names, then left him standing there alone. Joseph had suffered even more. His brothers had called him names: *Tattletale, master of dreams, Father's favorite*. Timothy wondered how alone Joseph felt in the bottom of the pit. But then, his brothers had sold him as a slave. They valued twenty pieces of silver more than his life. *At least my friends didn't sell me*, Timothy thought.

As Timothy arrived at the city gates, he looked at the beggars stretched across the steps to the Temple of Zeus. The same faces were there every day, looking for help from a false god. There would be no miracle for these people. Zeus had no power to restore their health or to make them rich. He could not hear their prayers or even see their needs. These people were all looking for help in the wrong place. There was no power here. Only God could heal their wounds and make them whole. Timothy turned and continued past the gates and down the hill.

Somewhere, deep inside his heart, Timothy knew that somehow God wanted to heal these people. God could make them whole. Timothy wanted to be part of that. "I will follow you even if my friends reject me. I will follow wherever you lead," he whispered.

Chapter 8

New Friends

There were few others working in the fields when Timothy arrived. Harvest wouldn't truly come for another month. Those in the fields now were either harvesting early grains or collecting grasses to dry like himself. Now nearly midmorning, Timothy had work to do. The sun had passed its high point when he finally stopped. He had stacked the basket so full that Timothy was unsure if he could manage to carry it alone. He stopped for a sip of water, then walked to the shade of a nearby tree. Another man, older than Timothy by about ten years, was already sitting under the tree. Timothy greeted him, "It's almost too hot to be working today."

"That it is, my friend. Come sit down. My name's Vitas," called the stranger-turned-acquaintance. He motioned to a place next to him and Timothy took a seat.

"I'm Timothy," he said as he sat down and pulled out the small bundle his mother had given him that morning. Timothy was glad when he opened it and saw several small loaves. "Share these with me. My mother sent far more than I can eat alone." Timothy held out two loaves.

"Thank you," Vitas replied as he took the bread. "Here, try some of this cheese." Vitas handed Timothy a chunk of soft goat cheese. The two sat in silence as they ate. Timothy watched the man. His brow was dripping with sweat, as was his own. The sun was hot overhead and working in the fields did nothing to diminish its intensity. Even here in the shade there was not much relief. Timothy looked around. He could see several piles stacked in the vicinity. None was as large as his own, but there were five, no, six of them.

"Are all of these stacks yours?" Timothy questioned, motioning toward the freshly cut stacks.

"Yeah," Vitas replied, "I've been out here since before the sun came up this morning. I'm adding a new room to my house and need the straw for the bricks and for the roof. Two more stacks should be enough, then I'll need to carry them back into the city." Vitas looked at Timothy. "And you, what are you doing with yours?"

"I'm replacing the stuffing in bed mattresses for my family," replied Timothy. He looked again at the man next to him, then to the piles of straw in the field. "Let me help you carry your stacks back into the city. The work would be easier with my help."

"Oh no, young sir, you have your own work to do."

"I can come back tomorrow. You have other work to do," Timothy responded. "Let me help you."

Vitas looked at Timothy. The work would be easier with help. "I still need to cut two more stacks, then you can help me."

"You can have my stack, it's more than enough. Let's go!" Timothy jumped to his feet and started toward the stacks.

"Wait for me! You don't know where I live," shouted Vitas hurrying to catch up with Timothy.

*

Several hours later Vitas and Timothy had finished transporting the straw. As Timothy dumped the last basketful onto the pile, he fell onto the heaping mound next to Vitas. Rhea, Vitas' wife, brought water to them. Both men greedily gulped the water. "Look at the two of you, one might think you'd never seen water before," Rhea joked. She smiled then turned to go back into the house.

"Thank you, Timothy," Vitas said. "You've proven to be a true friend today."

Not only had Timothy helped Vitas carry the straw, but they had talked and joked all afternoon. Timothy had shared about his family and Vitas had shared about his. Vitas and his wife had been married just two years. She was younger than him, closer to Timothy's age. They were soon expecting a baby. Vitas was hoping for a boy. The room he was building was not for the baby, however, but for the other member of their family, Vitas' cousin, Horace. Horace was a cripple who stayed by the Temple of Zeus all day, begging for alms. He had been born crippled, but now his parents had died and there was no other family that could care for him. "You must stay for dinner. It's the least we can do for all of your help."

"I am a bit hungry," Timothy replied.

"It's settled." Then toward the house Vitas called, "Rhea, Timothy's joining us for dinner."

"Delightful," she replied, calling from inside the small house. "Don't forget to bring your cousin home."

"We're going now," Vitas called. He had forgotten. "Come with me."

They walked together to the entrance of the city. Many others were coming back into the city from the fields now. Vitas walked up the steps of the temple toward a small, thin man easily twice Timothy's age, judging from the spots of grey in his hair. "Timothy, this is my cousin Horace. Horace, this is our new friend, Timothy." Timothy said a quick hello, then Vitas lifted Horace in his arms and the three men headed back toward dinner. Horace did not say a word, but eyed Timothy suspiciously.

When they arrived back at the house, the food was ready. They sat together on the floor and ate. The food was simple but filling. This meal only made Timothy more grateful for the delicious food his mother prepared every day. Vitas shared the story of how he and Timothy had met. Rhea thanked Timothy by giving him a second helping. Horace ate quietly, just watching Timothy. Eventually, the conversation slowed. Timothy looked around. In many ways the house was like his own. The room they were in was only half the size of the one in his own home, but the entryway had been larger and there were goats in the stall here. There was only one bedroom off the entryway, but Vitas had said that he was adding a second.

Timothy finished eating then excused himself, saying, "I need to be getting home, my mother and grandmother will worry if I'm not home soon." In truth, they were probably already worried, but Timothy didn't want to alarm his new friends. Vitas rose and walked Timothy to the front gate.

"Thank you again for your help today," Vitas began, "but can I ask you something? Why did you help me? You didn't know me or have any reason I can find to help me."

"I helped you because you needed help and my God wants me to help my neighbors and strangers alike," Timothy responded.

Vitas was silent, then answered, "Let me help you tomorrow. We'll cut what you need and then carry it back to your home together."

Timothy thought for a moment. He enjoyed the company of this new friend. "Agreed. I'll come by first thing in the morning and we can walk out together."

"Great! I'll see you tomorrow. And give my apologies to your mother if we kept you too late."

"See you tomorrow," Timothy replied, then turned toward home. He quickly made his way across the city. The sun had already gone down and the moon was shining in the sky. Candlelight from homes shone across the streets. When he arrived home, he dropped his things near the empty stall then went inside to find his mother. She was by the fire.

"Timothy, where have you been? I thought you went to gather straw. Are you okay?" Eunice questioned her son rapidly.

"Of course, he's okay," Lois interjected from the other side of the room. "Does he look like he's hurt? Look at him, he's smiling."

"That still doesn't explain why he came home with an empty basket," Eunice responded to her mother. The smile disappeared from Timothy's face confirming his mother's suspicions. Then, turning away her nose, "Or why he smells like a goat." She turned back to Timothy without breaking stride, "Go out back and wash up."

"You didn't even ask him if he ate, ask him if he ate something." Lois chided her daughter.

"If he comes home this late, I should hope that he had something to eat. And if not, I sent him enough bread this morning that he won't starve."

Timothy crossed the room to his mother. "I'm sorry I'm late, *Immah*. I'll go wash up and then tell you everything that happened." He leaned in to kiss her cheek. She pretended that she was mad at him, but the reality was that she was glad he was home.

"Mm-hmm," Eunice said as Timothy kissed her, "and leave those clothes outside too. They stink. I'll wash them tomorrow."

Timothy went to his room and grabbed a change of clothes, then went around to the back side of the house where a barrel sat, filled with rainwater. Timothy quickly washed himself, changed his clothes, then went back inside.

"Now, about what happened today," Eunice said as she handed Timothy a plate of food. It was still warm. Timothy took the plate and began to tell them about all that had happened. He told how he had worked, met Vitas, then helped him. He told about Vitas' family, Rhea and Horace, plus the little baby on the way. He told how they had invited him to stay for dinner and how it would have been impolite to refuse. He emphasized how much he preferred his mother's cooking. And he told how he was going tomorrow with Vitas to cut more straw.

"I know I was upset this morning about how things went with my friends, but God gave me another opportunity today with Vitas. I'm going to show him God through my actions and if I can, I'll use my words too," Timothy concluded. "That's what Joseph did after his brothers sold him. Joseph was a slave, but he proved to be faithful in every matter in the Egyptian's house. God sent Joseph to Egypt and, I believe today, God sent me to Vitas."

"So now you're like Joseph?" Lois questioned.

"No," Timothy replied, "I've not gone through anything like what he did, but I think I'm beginning to understand the purpose of his story and life. God allowed Joseph to be sold as a slave, then to be lied about and thrown into prison. Terrible things happened to Joseph not because he was a bad person, but because God could trust him to do what was right. Joseph would be a faithful testimony for God wherever he was. When Joseph served as a slave, the Egyptian saw that God was with him and the Lord made him to prosper. When the Egyptian's wife tried to seduce Joseph, he fled from evil. When Joseph was in prison, the guard trusted him to keep all that was there. Joseph did not allow his circumstances to determine his actions. He based his actions on what was faithful to God.

"I can do that too. If my friends reject me or God, it doesn't mean that God has rejected me. If something bad happens to me or to my family, I will continue to choose to do what is right. God has placed us here to be a light, so a light I will be."

Chapter 9

Witness

When Timothy woke the next morning, he quickly gathered his things then headed for the door. His nose demanded a detour when he smelled fresh bread baking in the kitchen. His mother was already awake and busy. She stopped her work when she saw Timothy in the doorway. "I thought you could invite your new friends to dinner tonight. If you want to, that is," Eunice said with a smile. She pulled several hot buns out of the small bread oven and wrapped them in a cloth. Timothy took them gratefully.

"Thanks, *Immah*. I'll ask them and let you know. We should be back with some straw by midday," Timothy replied. He dropped the buns safely into his bag, then started for Vitas' house. When he arrived, Vitas was just finishing with the goats.

"Good morning!" Timothy called.

"Good morning! Right on time. Let me take this milk to Rhea and then we can go." Vitas took the bucket into the kitchen, then returned a moment later with his bag already slung around his shoulder. "Can you carry my basket, at least until we reach the gates? I need to carry Horace with us."

"Sure, let me tie it on in front." Timothy's own basket was attached to his back. The baskets were not heavy, simply awkward because of their size. Vitas helped secure the second basket in front, balanced by Timothy's in the back. "My mother said that all three of you are invited to dinner with us tonight." Then he added with a smile, "She's already fixing the food, so you can't say no."

"That sounds great. I'll tell Rhea. I'm sure she'll be happy." Vitas went back into the kitchen and returned with Horace in his arms. Rhea followed right behind them.

"Hello, Timothy. Are you sure your mother wants all of us to come? We can be quite the crowd," Rhea said.

"She said she's fixing dinner for you. That means if I come to dinner without you, I might not get anything to eat. So, promise me you'll come," Timothy said with a smile.

"We'll be there," Rhea replied.

With the meal plans settled, the three men set off for the Temple of Zeus. Timothy tripped as a stray dog raced across his path but managed to regain his balance before he fell. They reached the Temple of Zeus without further incident and Vitas left Horace on the steps.

"I'll be back to get you when we finish in the fields," Vitas said to Horace.

Horace returned a look of indifference. Vitas untied his basket from Timothy and the two men began their way into the fields.

"I don't know what to do with him," Vitas complained. "He gives no respect to me or to Rhea. He's only been with us four months, but you would think that he could be a bit kinder to the people who take care of him. I thought that adding an extra room might soften him a bit, but if anything, it has made him even more sullen. He used to at least say 'Good morning' or 'Thank you,' but now if we get a grunt..."

"Yeah, I wanted to ask you about him. Has he always been this way?" Timothy asked.

“I grew up not too far from him, but I never really knew him as a kid. He was older and we all stayed away from him. I suppose we thought he was just some kind of a freak. I moved here about ten years ago and hadn’t really seen him until he moved in with us. It’s true, I’ve never heard him say more than a couple of words at a time, but I don’t remember him being like this. He got worse after his father, my uncle, died. After living his whole life with my uncle, Horace has lived with several different relatives. My other cousin, Horace’s brother, kept him for a couple of months, then my aunt kept him, then my parents. He’s been here the longest. They all live in Derbe, so we thought that moving him here might be better. At least it would be a change of scenery. I tried to find someone else that would take him after we found out Rhea was pregnant, but none of the rest of the family wanted him. That’s probably why he’s been so rude to you. I’m sure he expects that I’ll pass him off to you. Not that I would, but he doesn’t know that. Rhea said we would figure it out, but she’s too kind by far. Anyway, I’ve decided to try and make the best of it.”

“Sounds like you’re doing all you can,” Timothy replied. “Some people just need time. I know it took me a long time to get over my father’s death. There are still times when thinking about him makes me sad. At least I had my mother and grandmother to help me through it. I imagine Horace is the same, but from the sounds of it, he’s not really had anybody that he could trust. Trust has to be hard for him, given his situation. He’s so dependent on other people. It can’t be easy to have to rely on others so much. Show him that he can trust you and that your home is his home. Give him time. I think he’ll come around.”

“You sound exactly like Rhea. That’s the same thing she keeps saying. She says that he’s tired of being passed from one family member to the next and is worried that we’ll do the same now with the baby coming,” Vitas shrugged. “Maybe you are right. Anyway, here we are. Let's put our packs over there," he said pointing out a tree not too far away, "then we can start cutting right here."

The two busily went about their business, cutting the grasses and stacking them in their baskets. Timothy mirrored Vitas, trying to keep pace with him. When Vitas swung his blade, Timothy swung his. When Vitas stacked his bundles, Timothy did as well. The faster Vitas moved, the faster Timothy moved. Sweat poured off both men as the sun rose high into the sky. Timothy was determined not to let either the sun or Vitas beat him. Timothy was moving as fast as he could, but Vitas kept pushing faster. At last, Vitas called out, "Enough! You're going to wear me out. Besides, I think this should be enough for what you need."

Timothy collapsed onto the mound of grass nearest him. He looked around. Each of them had cut three stacks almost as large as his own yesterday and the sun wasn't even at its highest yet. "You're right. It is enough. I don't think I could have kept up with you any longer anyway."

"You keep up with me? I was trying to keep up with you!" Vitas laughed. "Just promise you won't make me race you carrying all this back into the city."

"Agreed, no more racing. Let's go sit in the shade for a bit."

Timothy and Vitas walked over to the tree and sat down. Both men pulled out their packs and began eating. After a few moments, Vitas spoke, "You don't worship the Greek gods, do you?"

Timothy looked at Vitas. His face seemed sincere, like a friend. "No, my family are Jews. We worship the God of heaven."

"Hmm, what you said last night made me think. I've never heard anybody say what you said that their God wanted them to help others. Not that I've ever thought much about the gods, but I like what you said. People should help each other. The gods never seem to help anybody. Do you really think the gods care what we do?"

"No," Timothy began cautiously, "I don't think the gods care what we do. I don't think the gods exist. I believe that there is only one God, but I do believe He cares what we do. He cares because He made us. And He loves His creation."

"Well, the Greek gods certainly don't love us. They only love themselves," Vitas half-shouted toward the sky. Then in a quieter tone, "Is this God of heaven a new god? How does one learn more about Him?"

"No, He's not a new God. He is eternal, and people have worshiped Him since the beginning of time. The Hebrew people, my people, have worshiped Him for thousands of years. We also have God's written word, the Law, the Prophets, and the Writings. These Scriptures teach us God's law and tell us how to live, but most importantly, they reveal God to us."

"Can anyone learn about your God? Or do we have to be Jews, like you?" Vitas asked.

"He's the God of heaven, not the God of Jews. All who are under heaven may come to Him and live," Timothy answered.

"I want to learn more about your God. Will you teach me?" Vitas asked.

"Me? I'm too young to teach you," replied Timothy.

"I've already learned enough from you that I know I'd rather have your God than any of the Greek gods," Vitas responded.

Timothy thought for a moment, then replied, "I'll teach you everything I can, but if I can't teach you then you have to learn from someone else. Okay?"

"Okay," came the answer. "But for now, let's get busy carrying all of this back to your house."

"Sounds like a plan. And no racing, right?"

"Right, no racing," Vitas smiled.

The two men busied themselves packing the baskets, and before long were on their way back into the city. A couple short hours later they had carried all the grasses back to Timothy's house and deposited them in the goat stall.

"You know, this stall should be filled with goats, not hay," Vitas chided Timothy.

"I know. We used to have some when I was little. I know my mother would like to have the milk again."

"What are the two of you talking about out here?" Eunice asked as she came into the courtyard.

"I was just telling Timothy I needed to get back home."

"You're leaving so soon?" she replied.

"There's a couple things I need to take care of before we come back this evening," Vitas answered Eunice. "But don't worry, we'll be back. The smells from your kitchen are too good for me to miss it. We'll be here around sundown?"

"That would be lovely," Eunice replied, smiling at the compliment.

Timothy walked Vitas to the gate. When he returned, his mother said, "You finished quickly today."

"I couldn't have done it without Vitas." Timothy looked at his mother, then across the room at his grandmother. "You know, He asked me about God today. I knew God wanted me to be a light for Him. It was completely different from when I talked to my friends. They didn't want to hear anything I said, but Vitas listened to everything. I told him about God and that the Greek gods aren't real. Now, he wants to learn more about God. He even said he wants me to teach him!"

"So now our Joseph has left the prison and entered Pharaoh's court. Is that it?" Lois interjected with a smile.

"I guess," Timothy chuckled. "It doesn't really compare because Joseph went through so much more. I didn't interpret any dreams or make any plans for a famine. All I did was cut some straw, but it does feel different having someone actually listen when I talk about God. Joseph's brothers rejected him and his message, like my friends did to me. But Vitas listened just like Pharaoh did with Joseph."

"And just like Joseph, you chose to do right," Lois said. "You never know where the path of faith will lead, but you do know who made the path and walks it with you. Timothy, remember to allow your faith to lead you, not the circumstances that surround you, and you'll do just fine," Lois challenged.

"But for now, how about you go clean up," Eunice said. "Your friends are going to be here soon."

Chapter 10

The Plan

"We looked everywhere for him. My husband was out in the street, asking neighbors if they had seen him. I had looked everywhere in the house, under everything. We were all calling his name, 'Timothy! Timothy!' But no one could find him," Eunice told the story.

"How old did you say he was?" Vitas asked.

"He was only four. He was so little I was afraid that he was stuck somewhere, or worse, hurt. He loved to climb. My husband had even gone up to the roof to see if he had climbed up there."

"Do we have to tell this story? It's so embarrassing. I'm never bringing anybody over for dinner again," Timothy said while burying his face in his hands. Everybody laughed.

"So where did you find him?" asked Rhea.

"My mother asked if anybody had checked the goats," Eunice replied. "We still had goats back then. In fact, our doe had just given birth a month or so before. So, I peeked into the stall, but I didn't see anything because it was dark," Eunice continued. "I saw the doe snuggled with its kid over in the corner. I climbed into the pen and went for a closer look. That's when I saw him. Timothy was sound asleep snuggled right up against the goats. He had climbed in to play with the baby and had fallen asleep with it. The doe wouldn't even let me get close enough to take him away. I'm not sure whether she thought I was trying to take her baby or mine. Then when I did get him, he started crying because he wanted to go back with the goats!"

"A regular little goat!" Vitas exclaimed. He slapped Timothy on the back, but this only made his face turn a brighter shade of red. Everyone laughed. Finally, even Timothy conceded that it was a cute story.

"But we never have to tell it again? Right?"

"Not until you decide to get married, then I'll make sure to tell it again," Lois proclaimed.

The evening had gone perfectly. Dinner had long since finished and both families gathered around the fireplace reclining against the cushions. The conversation all evening made it feel as if they had been old family friends forever. Vitas had regaled them all with the story of how he met Rhea; how he had convinced her father to allow them to marry. Eunice and Lois in turn had told stories of their children, offering bits of advice for the soon-to-be parents. Though the candles were nearly spent, no one seemed eager for the night to finish. Even Horace, who had seemed uninterested in everything at first, was now following the conversation. He had even laughed a couple times.

"I don't know why, but I was nervous about coming over tonight," Rhea began. "Timothy was so nice to Vitas, helping him in the fields. I should have known that the women who raised such a good son would be just as nice."

"Thank you, Rhea," Eunice replied, "That means a lot to me. I know you'll raise your child just the same."

"I hope so, but sometimes I am so scared," Rhea replied. "You don't seem to be scared at all."

"It's because of their God. Their God is good," Vitas interjected. "I told you that's why Timothy helped me. It's because their God is better than our gods."

"I was going to say, it's because I have more years of experience," Eunice smiled, "but what Vitas says isn't wrong. Our God is good. It doesn't mean that bad things won't happen, but it does mean that God has a plan and is with us through all the bad that does happen."

"What do you mean, God has a plan and is with you?" Horace asked. Everybody turned to look at Horace. Vitas' mouth was slightly agape. Silence filled the air. Horace repeated, slowly this time, "What do you mean, God has a plan and is with you?"

Eunice looked around the room at each person, then back at Horace. She could see the desperation in his eyes. He genuinely wanted to know; they all did. "Can I tell you a story? It's a story of our people and our God. I think it'll help you understand." Horace looked deep into her eyes and without a word, began nodding his head.

"Joseph was one of the earliest fathers of our people. It was his father, Israel, who gave his name to our people and our land. Israel had twelve sons, but Joseph was the most favored. He wasn't the oldest, eleventh in line actually, but he was the oldest son of Israel's favorite wife, Rachel. Rachel only had two sons, Joseph and Benjamin. She died giving birth to Benjamin. Because of his love for Rachel, Israel loved Joseph more than the others and he gave Joseph a beautiful coat of many colors. This favor on Joseph provoked the jealousy of the other brothers. God also gave Joseph visions where the rest of the family bowed before him. These visions did nothing to gain the brothers' favor but provoked only more jealousy. Through all this Joseph continued faithfully. He honored his father and obeyed his word. It was this obedience that would cost him.

"One day Israel sent Joseph after his brothers. His older brothers had taken the sheep to find pasture. Israel wanted to know where and how they were. Joseph looked for his brothers, and after several days, found them. But his brothers conspired to kill him. They first cast him into a pit where they were going to leave him to die. Then a caravan of traders came, and the brothers decided to sell Joseph as a slave. They did this for twenty pieces of silver. The brothers took Joseph's coat, the sign of their father's favor, and made it look like a wild beast had caught Joseph and killed him. They took it back to Israel with the story that they had found it on the road home."

"That's horrible!" Rhea exclaimed. "How could people do such a thing, not only to their brother, but to their father?"

"It's no different than people today," Lois replied. "We see people sold to fight in the arena and betrayed by their own all the time. And for what, a bit of silver?"

"I suppose you're right, but I interrupted your story," Rhea said. "Forgive me. Please, go on."

"Meanwhile, Joseph was taken to Egypt as a slave," Eunice continued. "There he served in the house of an Egyptian, an officer of the pharaoh. Joseph served faithfully and God blessed the house of the Egyptian for Joseph's sake. Even then, the day came that Joseph was betrayed yet again. The Egyptian's wife desired to be with Joseph, but he denied her advances. Finally, she lied that he had forced himself on her and the Egyptian cast Joseph into prison. Even there, God blessed Joseph and made him to prosper. The keeper of the prison gave Joseph authority over all the prison during his time there.

"While in prison, God allowed Joseph to interpret the dreams of two prisoners, a baker and the king's cupbearer. Both interpretations came true and, just as Joseph said, Pharaoh killed the baker but restored the cupbearer to his position. Yet Joseph remained in prison for another two years. Then the king of Egypt had a dream. None of his wise men could give the interpretation of his dreams. Only after this did the cupbearer remember Joseph. He told Pharaoh about the man in prison that had interpreted his own dream. The king brought Joseph before him and again God gave Joseph the interpretation of the dreams.

"Joseph told Pharaoh that the land would experience seven years of plenty followed by seven years of famine. Joseph told the king to set someone over the land to store the harvest so that there would be food to last the seven years of famine. Pharaoh placed Joseph in that position."

"Ha! I knew it," Vitas exclaimed. "I knew there would be a happy ending."

"Ah, but this isn't the ending. Joseph still hasn't reached the end of the journey," Eunice answered. "You see, Joseph busied Egypt collecting and storing grain for the famine that would come. And the famine did come, but not to Egypt alone. The famine came to all the nations around her, including the land of Israel and the rest of Joseph's family. It was then that his brothers came to Egypt to buy grain."

"And Joseph took them as slaves, didn't he?" Vitas asked.

"Will you be quiet already?" Rhea said, poking her husband in the side.

"Owww! What was that for?"

"Some of us want to hear the rest of the story. You keep interrupting and your child will get here before she can finish," Rhea said while rubbing her belly. Then she turned to Eunice, "You can continue, my husband will keep his questions for the end." Timothy slapped Vitas on the back and laughed. Vitas opened his mouth to respond, but the look on Rhea's face stopped him. As he shut his mouth, they all burst into laughter.

As the laughter subsided, Eunice continued, "No, Joseph didn't make his brothers slaves. But he didn't reveal himself to them immediately either. By this time, Joseph had been in Egypt for many years. He dressed as an Egyptian, he spoke as an Egyptian, and, to his brother's eyes, he seemed to be an Egyptian. They did not recognize him. But Joseph knew them.

He accused them of being spies, come to examine the land. They replied that they were only twelve brothers, come for grain. Because they were but ten in number, they told Joseph that one brother had died and their father had kept the youngest at home. Joseph told them he would only believe them if they came with the other brother, then he locked all of them in prison for three days.

"After three days he brought the brothers before him again. He told them he would let them go with their grain, but they could not return without the youngest brother. As they stood before him, Joseph's brothers argued with each other saying that all of this was because of their sin against their brother. Joseph heard all that they said but gave no sign that he understood their language. Then he kept one of the brothers captive as a guarantee of their return. When they left, he instructed the servants to return their money in their bags with the grain."

"It must have been so hard for Joseph. To keep secret who he really was," Rhea now proclaimed.

"Hey, I thought we were saving our comments for the end," Vitas prodded gently. "But besides that, the brothers got what they deserved. After what they had done, Joseph should have killed them."

"Maybe he should have. He probably could have if that had been his desire," Eunice continued. "But he wanted to see if they had changed. And he wanted to see his brother and his father. So, he sent his nine brothers back home. They found the money with the grain and were scared that the Egyptians would accuse them of stealing now. They told their father all that had happened, and that Benjamin must return with them, but Israel would not allow it. Finally, when the food was gone, he relented. Judah, one of the brothers, told his father that he would give his own life in the place of Benjamin's if need be. So, the brothers left for Egypt once again. This time they brought gifts and double the money as they intended to repay the debt from the first trip.

"When they arrived in Egypt, Joseph prepared a great feast for them in his own home. Like Vitas, they were sure that the Egyptian meant to make them his slaves. They even told Joseph's servant that they had found their money in their bags, but he said they had found a treasure from their God. They owed nothing. At the feast, Joseph had them arranged by order of birth and served Benjamin a portion five times the rest of them.

"Then Joseph prepared one final test. He returned all their money in their sacks again and placed his own cup in Benjamin's sack. Then he sent them on their way. As soon as they had left the city, Joseph sent his men after them. The soldiers accused the brothers of theft. Whoever had the cup would become a slave to the Egyptian. Of course, they found the cup in Benjamin's sack. All the brothers were distraught. They all returned to Joseph and begged forgiveness. Joseph said they could all go home, only the one who had the cup must stay. Judah stood before Joseph and pled his case. He had promised his father to return Benjamin alive. Then he offered himself in Benjamin's place.

"At this, Joseph sent everyone else out of the room. Only he and his brothers remained. He began to cry. Then he said, 'I am Joseph. Is my father still alive?' His brothers were in shock. They couldn't believe it. Joseph told them that he wasn't upset. He forgave them. What they had meant for evil, God meant for good. Joseph knew that God had sent him ahead to preserve life. He sent them home in peace with instructions to move the whole family to Egypt. Israel didn't believe them at first, but when he saw all the treasure Joseph had given his brothers, he too believed. The reunion of Joseph and Israel was one of the greatest in history."

"Wow," Vitas whispered, "he forgave them. After all he had suffered because of them, he forgave them."

"Because Joseph saw the plan of God and knew that God was with him wherever the path led," Timothy replied. "God can use anyone or anything to do something good."

"Anyone?" The question came from Horace, but all eyes were fixed on Timothy.

"Anyone," Timothy replied.

"Anyone," echoed Eunice and Lois.

Chapter 11

Deliverer

"So, was Moses some kind of demigod?" Rhea asked as she tried to make sense of the story Timothy had been telling. Almost every day for the past two weeks he had come to their home with new stories about God and his people. She liked the creation story best so far. She liked how God made men and women special. That God cared for people in such a personal way made Him seem more real than the gods she had once worshipped. However, this latest story had her confused.

"No, Rhea, there are no demigods, just the same as there are no gods," Vitas answered before Timothy could. Then turning to Timothy, "That's right, isn't it?"

"That's right. There are no demigods or gods. There is one God and He is the one who gave Moses the ability to do such things," Timothy answered. "The truth is that Moses was a man, a prophet chosen by God, but still only a man. God called him to deliver His people from Egypt. The miracles he performed and the plagues that came upon Egypt were not from Moses, but from God. From the Nile river turning to blood to the three days of darkness, each one was a display of God's power over the gods of Egypt."

Timothy and Vitas stepped back from the wall. They had been working all day every day for over a week. Both men were exhausted, but it would be worth it when they finished the job. Soon they would finish the new room and Horace could move into it. They had just finished the walls, now only the roof needed to be completed.

"Horace, what do you think?" Vitas asked.

"It's wonderful. It really is," he responded. Ever since the dinner at Timothy's house, something had changed with Horace. He was still quiet and occasionally cranky, but there was a different spirit about him. When Timothy started coming to share more stories about God, Horace had asked to stay home rather than have Vitas take him to the temple. "Would you take me inside, so I can see it from there?"

"It's not finished yet. There's no roof, and we haven't moved in your bed or anything yet," Vitas replied.

"That's okay. I only want to see."

Vitas walked over to where Horace was sitting and picked him up in his arms. He carried him into the new room. "I was thinking we could put your bed against this wall and…"

"It's perfect," Horace interrupted. "Thank you."

"I'm glad you like it. We should be able to finish the roof in a couple days and then you can move in." Vitas carried Horace back out to the courtyard and placed him on his cushion. Then he turned back to Timothy, "As I count it, there should be one more."

Timothy looked at Vitas, "One more? You want to make another room?"

"No, not another room," Vitas chuckled, "another plague. I only counted nine plagues and you said there were ten of them."

"He's right, Timothy," Rhea added. Then she listed as she counted on her fingers, "Water to blood, frogs, gnats, flies, the animals died, boils, hail, locusts, and darkness. Nine. You missed one."

"No, it's not missing," Timothy replied with a smile. "I just haven't told you about the last one yet."

"Well, out with it. Don't keep us in suspense any longer," Vitas responded.

"The last one was the most important one. The final plague was the one that would deliver the Hebrews out of Egypt. God had shown his power over all the gods of Egypt. Except one–Pharaoh. Pharaoh was the man-god. He was king of all Egypt and still refused to bow before the God of heaven. So, the tenth plague must show God's power over Pharaoh. The last plague was the death of the firstborn. The firstborn of every family would die. It didn't matter if you were a slave or the king, this was God's final judgment on Egypt."

"God killed the firstborn of every family, including Israel's?" Rhea questioned.

"It's the curse of sin that all people should perish. It's been that way since Adam. But yes, God said that all the firstborn would be killed. This would be His final judgement on the gods of Egypt. But just as He did with Adam, He made a way of escape; He sent a deliverer. As God taught Adam to offer a sacrifice for sin, so God instructed Moses to offer a sacrifice. Each family was to offer a lamb. If they were too poor for a lamb, they were to share one with a neighbor. They would eat the lamb as their last meal in Egypt, but more importantly, they were to put the blood on the doorposts, on both sides and above the door. This would be a sign of their faith in God and their obedience to Him. That night when the Lord came to visit Egypt, He saw the blood on the door and passed over the house. But at every house where the people had not marked the door with blood, death came to the firstborn. That night a great cry came over the land of Egypt. And the king's palace was no different from the servant's home. Even Pharaoh's firstborn died. In his sorrow and in his defeat, he sent Israel away."

"I would have too. If the Hebrew God had so thoroughly destroyed my nation and brought death to my land, I would have wanted them gone too," Vitas responded.

Horace spoke up, "I would have gone with them. If I had seen all of that, I would have been convinced that their God was the true God and I would have followed Him too."

"That's kind of what we are doing now, isn't it? Following the true God?" asked Rhea.

"You're right, Rhea," Timothy answered. "And there were those in Egypt who thought exactly like you, Horace. The Scriptures tell us that when Moses and the people left, there was a mixed multitude that followed them. I like to think they were neighbors or even enemies who had been convinced of the truth of God. Maybe they were like my parents, families that had married Jews and come to believe in the true God. Regardless of who they were, this mixed multitude followed after Moses."

"I like this God more and more. He shows His power, then He forgives and accepts those who come to Him," Vitas stated. "It's like when He promised to Abraham that all families of the earth would be blessed. He made your people a light to shine to the rest of the world. Some of the Egyptians saw that light and followed."

"So, Moses wasn't a demigod. He was the deliverer," Rhea stated.

"Yeah, in a way," Timothy answered. "God sent Moses to be His voice and to lead His people, but I think the lamb was the real deliverer. Without the sacrifice, there was no deliverance from the judgment of sin. That's what we celebrate every year when we celebrate Passover."

"You celebrate this every year?" Vitas asked excitedly.

"It's only the biggest holiday of the year for us," Timothy smiled. "We have other holidays, but the Passover is the most important. It reminds us of the sacrifice that we must make to cover the penalty of our sin. It's a week-long celebration."

"A week long?" Vitas replied. "Please, tell me it's coming soon. We want to celebrate too."

"Well, it's actually not until next spring," Timothy responded sadly. "But I can teach you all about it before then. And Rhea, my mother can teach you all about the special foods that we prepare."

"Special foods? I like the sound of that!" Vitas was practically glowing. "This is definitely better than the Greek gods. Let me guess, we eat lamb, just like they did in Egypt. I love lamb."

"Oh, so now we base our religion on who has the best food?" questioned Rhea.

"Of course not," Vitas responded. "But it doesn't hurt to have a God who enjoys a good holiday," he added with a smile.

"I agree with Vitas on this one," Timothy added with a laugh. "A holiday is a good thing. Especially one with such a good meaning."

"I suppose you're right," Rhea answered. Then looking around she said, "Well, are you just going to stand there and let this pregnant woman finish everything or are you going to help me clean up this mess?"

"I think I heard your mother calling, Timothy," Vitas laughed. "You hurry home and I'll take care of the mess." Vitas turned toward his wife with a smile. He held out his muddy hands and started toward her.

"No, you don't! Get away from me. You're filthy!" Rhea squealed as Vitas grabbed her up in his arms. "Put me down!" Vitas carried her into the house where the sound of their laughter carried into the courtyard.

Timothy laughed as he picked up the few tools left on the ground. "Are they always like this?" he asked Horace.

"Most of the time," Horace answered. "Vitas likes to laugh. That's a good thing." His voice trailed off, then he looked up at Timothy. "Thank you," Horace whispered.

"For what?" A puzzled look crossed Timothy's face.

"I was rude when we first met," Horace answered. "I don't like new people. My experience has...not been good. But you're not like most people. You've been kind to me, even though I was rude."

"You're not like most people either," Timothy answered.

"Yeah, I know," Horace replied. "Most people can walk."

"There's that," Timothy said, "but I was thinking about something else. You see things differently than other people. You see things others miss. Vitas was ready to let Israel leave Egypt, but you wanted to go with them. That has nothing to do with your legs. It has to do with your faith."

"Yeah," Horace said. "I never thought of it that way. I guess God sees me the same way, by my faith, not my legs. Right?"

"Moses said to love the Lord your God with all your heart, soul, and might. He didn't say anything about legs," Timothy answered with a smile.

"Heart, soul, and might. I like that," Horace said.

Chapter 12

Manna

When Timothy arrived home, he could hear his mother and grandmother talking with someone. Timothy listened for a moment, then when he heard the voice he rushed inside. "Uncle Carpus, it's so good to see you. How have you been?"

"Timothy, my boy!" Carpus shouted. "Come over here. Let me see you." Uncle Carpus wasn't really Timothy's uncle, even though he might as well have been. Timothy couldn't remember a time when he didn't know Uncle Carpus. He was a friend of Timothy's father and had checked on the family since his friend's death. Eunice liked Carpus simply because he was Jewish and provided another connection for her son to that part of his heritage. Lois, however, never seemed to stop arguing with him. Even now it was clear on her face that she was unhappy about something.

"You're getting taller by the day. You look just like your father. Looks like you've been busy working today," Carpus said embracing Timothy by the shoulders.

"I've been helping some friends add an extra room in their house," Timothy replied.

"Strong, diligent, hardworking, and helpful. Precisely what I'm looking for," Carpus continued as he turned back toward Eunice. "I tell you, he's right for it."

"It's his decision," she replied. "You should ask him."

"Come, my boy, sit down." Uncle Carpus led Timothy over toward the fireplace where they reclined against the large cushions. "I've just explained to your mother and grandmother my offer. I'll explain it to you exactly as I did to them."

"Hmph," came the grunt from Lois in her chair on the other side of the room. Eunice hushed her mother. Lois crossed her arms and turned away toward the open window.

Uncle Carpus continued unabated with the smoothness of someone who sells things for a living, "As you know, I sell spices in the market. What you may not know is that my son and his family have moved to Iconium. He decided that he doesn't want to wait for his old man to die, so he's gone there to open his own spice shop. Now, don't misunderstand me, I'm happy that he's going out on his own. He's more than capable. After all, I did teach him everything he knows. But he wants adventure in the big city. Not me, I've done that. I'm happy here in my own little corner of the world. Nice, quiet little Lystra. That's all I need.

"But my son moving to Iconium has left me in a spot. You see, I depend on my son and grandson to help with the shop. Usually, my son goes with me to Iconium to purchase spices, and my grandson helps with things around the shop. Mind you, not anything too difficult. Mostly cleaning up and lifting some of the larger sacks. My back isn't what it used to be. So, I find myself in need of some good strong help.

"I was at home talking to my wife about this when I remembered my dear friend and his son Timothy. I promised your father I'd look after you if anything should ever happen to him. So, I came right over here to talk it over with you. What do you say? Mind you, I cannot offer you a proper apprenticeship, but I'll help you learn whatever I can. You'd have to help around the shop and go with me to Iconium once a month. Are you good with numbers? Doesn't matter, I'll teach you to multiply and divide myself. Of course, I'd give you a fair stipend for your work. You won't get rich, son, but it'll help your mother around here. What do you say?" With that, Uncle Carpus finally paused and drew in a deep breath. He crossed his hands on top of his large belly and leaned back.

Timothy thought about what he had heard. It would help his mother if he did this. Going to Iconium once a month would be exciting as well. He didn't suppose the work that Uncle Carpus wanted him to do was all that difficult. Timothy looked to his mother, but Eunice's face was a blank slate. He could read nothing in her expression. His grandmother still faced the window. "Uncle Carpus, I think it sounds like a great offer, what you're proposing. Could I talk about it with my mother and grandmother tonight and let you know tomorrow?"

Carpus looked over Timothy. "You're a wise man too. Never buy what the merchant sells the first time around. I tell you, my boy, you'll not have to work on any Sabbath day and if your mother," then glancing toward Lois, "or grandmother, should have need of you, then family, of course, comes first. And I'll continue to provide your mother with whatever spices she needs, just as I always do." He waited a moment as he watched Timothy. Seeing that there would be no immediate answer he clapped his hands on his knees and rose to his feet. "Tomorrow it is!" he proclaimed.

Timothy rose with Carpus. He gave the old man a warm embrace, then walked with him toward the door. Eunice came over with a large loaf of bread. "Thank you, my dear," Carpus said as he received the gift. "Your bread is the finest in the whole Empire. Your hospitality has been lovely." Then half-shouting over his shoulder as he stepped out the door, "Good-bye, my dear Lois. It's been a pleasure as always." The old man stepped into the courtyard and Timothy joined him as they walked to the street together.

"I don't like that man," Lois grumbled when he had gone, "not even a little bit."

"*Immah*, everyone knows you don't like him. Even the spiders up in the corners know you don't like him," Eunice joked.

"There's no spiders up in the corners. I cleaned them out yesterday," fussed Lois. "But even spiders are better than that man."

"I don't know why you dislike him so much," replied Eunice. "He's been nothing but kind to us since my husband died. He's given us spices both for cooking and medicine. When you were sick, he never once charged us for the spices the doctor prescribed."

"It's his eyes. His eyes are shifty."

"His eyes are shifty? *Immah*," Eunice was exasperated. "So, you don't want Timothy to work for someone because his eyes are shifty. Are both eyes shifty, or is it just the one? Maybe his nose is too big, or his coat is too bright." Lois opened her mouth to interrupt, but Eunice kept going. "No, I know what it is, you just don't like the fact that someone is helping you and you can't do anything about it. I think maybe the problem isn't Carpus at all. Shifty eyes...

"No, *Immah*," Eunice exclaimed, "you act like everything is fine, like we're feasting on milk and honey. But we're not in the promised land, we're wandering around in the desert. You tell Timothy to trust God, but when God sends someone to help, you want to push them away. It's like you're waiting for God to part the waters when what we need is manna. You want to walk on dry ground with all the problems washed away, but we need water from the rock. We need clothes to wear and shoes to put on our feet, and I pray God will make them last as long as they did for our people when they wandered in the wilderness so long ago.

"We're like Israel after they left Egypt. Losing my husband and almost losing you; that was my Egypt. But God delivered us through all of that. I never want to forget God's goodness in getting us through those dark days. But here we are looking for what's next. We want to see the Red Sea part. We want the pillar of cloud and the pillar of fire. We're looking for the next big thing that God is going to do. And while we're here complaining about shifty eyes, God's busy sending manna. Sure, you may not like the form in which God provides, but He is providing the things that we need each and every day. The manna may taste different than you like but God sent it to nourish.

"Now, I know you don't like Carpus, but he is a good man, and he's Jewish. He will teach Timothy a trade, and he's doing it to be a blessing to us. Sure, he needs the help, but he doesn't have to do this, he could ask anyone. But God sent him to us because He knows we need it. So, if Timothy decides to do this, you won't say a word otherwise." Eunice stopped. Her mother nodded toward the open door. Eunice could see Timothy's shadow outside the opening.

"Timothy, you can come in," Eunice said.

A moment later Timothy sheepishly stuck his head into the room. "Is it safe?" he joked with a big smile. "Are you done telling *Sabta* how it's going to be?"

"How long have you been standing out there?" Eunice asked.

"Something about shifty eyes," Timothy replied. "I'm guessing Uncle Carpus, not me."

"Don't you start," Eunice answered, then shaking her head she muttered, "Shifty eyes…" Then looking up, she asked Timothy, "Well, you heard what I said. What do you want to do?"

Timothy waited a moment, then crossed the room to his grandmother. He knelt in front of her and took both her hands in his. Lois looked at Timothy and said, "Your mother's right. Exactly like God supplied food and water for His people in the desert, He provides for us the same. Sometimes God's blessing just falls from heaven, other times He gives you a job working for a man your grandmother doesn't like.

"God even made a way for those who complained to be made right," Lois continued glancing at Eunice to make sure she had heard. "See, complaining is in our blood. It's what our people do best. Our people complained about the long road, the lack of bread and water, and yes, even the manna. So, God sent snakes as a judgment of their ungratefulness. Instead of letting them die though, God told Moses to make a bronze snake to hang on a pole. All who looked at it were healed. It was not medicine that healed their bites, but their faith in God. I will learn to look at this the same. It's not the man that is helping us, but God who sent the man to help us. Who knows, I may even learn to tolerate the man." She smiled and nodded to Timothy as he squeezed her hands.

Timothy looked up to his mother, then stated, "Looks like I'm going to work for Uncle Carpus tomorrow."

Chapter 13

Obedience

Timothy awoke early the next morning and readied himself for the coming day. He dressed quickly then walked to the kitchen. The sun had not yet appeared on the horizon, yet his mother sat quietly by the fire tending the bread in the oven. Timothy sat next to her in the quiet stillness. He watched the coals as they glowed in the darkness. Eunice wrapped her arm around her son then began to pray, "O Lord, You are the light that illuminates our darkness. Your way is perfect, Your word is proven. You are the shield that protects us. Lead us on the path of integrity. You are our God and our rock, our strong fortress for today." Eunice pulled out some hot buns and handed them to her son. She took one for herself and together the two enjoyed the warm bread. When they had finished the buns, she pulled out several more, wrapped them in a cloth, then handed them to Timothy. "Now go. I'll see you tonight." Timothy kissed his mother on the cheek, placed the bundle in his pack, and silently slipped out into the darkness.

It was a short walk to the market, but by the time Timothy had arrived, the sun had already begun to peak above the horizon. The market here in Lystra was not large. It was an open square in the center of town surrounded by houses on all sides. To one side of the square was the vendor's market. Three rows of small booths were set up here. Each one had a bright canvas canopy to shade from the sun. One could find anything they needed here. Fruits and vegetables from the local fields, meat butchered fresh almost every day, leather and textiles in every color, shape, and size, as well as many types of pottery could all be bought or bartered. There were also several empty booths reserved for traveling merchants who came from Iconium, Antioch, or even Tarsus. They did not come frequently, but when they did the whole city would come to see the goods they would display. Small stone benches filled the other side of the square. That was where people gathered to discuss the latest happenings, trade the latest philosophies, or simply gossip about their neighbors.

Timothy headed for one of the houses just past the booths. Several of the homes that surrounded the plaza had been converted into shops. This was one of them. The front room overlooking the market was home to the spice shop, while Carpus' residence was in the back. The door was already propped open, so Timothy stepped inside. A thousand different smells assaulted Timothy's nose, some sweet, others sharper.

"Timothy, my boy!" exclaimed Carpus from his stool. "I knew you would come to help your dear old Uncle Carpus." He paused as he looked over Timothy, then asked, "You are here to help me, aren't you?"

"Yes, I've decided to come work for you. I've wanted to do more to help my mother and God brought you and your offer at just the right time." Timothy looked around. There were shelves lining all four walls of the room. Small jars lined the upper shelves while larger jars filled the lower ones. Dividing the room in half was a large counter, filled with what seemed to be a hundred different spices. Timothy recognized ginger, cloves, cinnamon, mustard, and his own favorite, pepper, but there were countless others that he had no idea what they were or how to use them. Timothy looked back to Carpus, then asked, "Where can I start?"

"Right to it, eh? I like that. No time for idle talk, just like me. Straight to work," Carpus rambled. "Come with me," he said as he rose to his feet. Carpus led Timothy into a small back room filled with large sacks and countless chests of various sizes which Timothy guessed were filled with even more spices. Carpus opened another door which led into the courtyard. There Timothy could see the rest of Carpus' home. It was much bigger than his own, mostly due to the addition of a second level. There was a stable with several stalls in the back. "Do you like animals, my boy?" Carpus asked as he headed for the stable.

Timothy had paused as he looked around. Now he hurried to catch up to Carpus as he was already halfway across the courtyard. "Yes, sir. We had goats when I was little," Timothy replied.

"Ah yes, I remember your father used to bring me goat's milk. Good man your father was. Good milk too, as I recall." Carpus paused as they reached the stable. "Now, I don't have goats, but I do have the emperor living here. Timothy, meet Claudius." Timothy looked at the donkey standing in the corner of the stable.

"You named your donkey after the emperor?" Timothy asked.

"Oh no, they named the emperor after my donkey," Carpus replied with a quick smile. Carpus chuckled at his own joke. Timothy had to smile as well. "Anyway, I need you to clean out the stable and the old emperor could use a bath as well. There's a pitchfork and a shovel in the corner over there," Carpus said. "We use the emperor's mess for fertilizer, so throw it in the cart. We can take it out to the fields when you're done. There's fresh straw in the last stall. I'll be out front in the shop if you need anything." With that, Carpus patted Timothy on the back and quickly walked back to the shop. Timothy looked at the stable. It looked like no one had cleaned it in a month, maybe more. Claudius was covered in filth as well. This was going to be a long day.

*

The sun was dipping below the horizon when Timothy finally made his way home. He had spent the whole morning cleaning the stable. Carpus had said the stalls had never been that clean even when they were first built. After a short break, Timothy had hitched Claudius to the cart, and then he and Carpus had gone out to the field to unload the cart. More precisely, Timothy had unloaded and spread the manure. Carpus had sat in the shade of the cart and talked about the importance of good fertilizer for the growth of good spices. He'd been extremely specific about where and how Timothy should place the fertilizer. Timothy was grateful to have finally finished. When they'd arrived back at the house, Timothy had scrubbed Claudius till he sparkled. He'd managed to wash the filth off himself as well, but the odor of the stables still remained. He slipped back to his room to change his clothes before he went in to see his mother and grandmother.

"There you are," Lois smiled. "I was beginning to wonder if that rascal was going to keep you all day."

"*Immah*!" Eunice turned to her mother. Eunice was finishing preparations for dinner.

"Fine, he's not a rascal," Lois submitted. Timothy kissed his mother's cheek, then went to kiss his grandmother's as well.

"What's that smell?" Eunice asked as Timothy walked away. "Do you smell it?"

Lois grabbed Timothy as he kissed her cheek. She sniffed him. "I smell it. It's Timothy! What is that smell? I don't recognize that spice."

"It's not a spice," Timothy responded. "It's Claudius."

"Who's Claudius?" Eunice asked.

"It's Uncle Carpus' donkey."

"I take it back. He is a rascal," Lois proclaimed. "I thought you were working in a spice shop, not the stables. I'm going over there right now."

"*Sabta*, sit down," Timothy calmed her. "This is what he needed done. He can't clean that stable himself. I doubt anybody has cleaned it since his son left. I knew that there would be things he needed me to do that required some hard work. I don't mind. It felt good to see Claudius all clean. He looked happy."

"He named his donkey Claudius?" Eunice asked, "after the emperor?"

"No," Timothy smiled, "they named the emperor after his donkey." Even Lois cracked a smile at that.

"You know," Eunice began, "sometimes God asks us to do things that aren't what we expect as well. We must learn to be flexible in our expectations as we remain obedient to God. We thought you were going to work with spices today and you ended up cleaning a stable. It's like when Joshua led the people into the promised land. They thought they were going to be attacking Jericho, but God appeared to Joshua and told him to walk around the city instead. God's plan was different than what they expected, but they obeyed anyway. They obeyed because they trusted God."

"Yeah, that's kind of how I felt today," Timothy answered. "I was a bit discouraged this morning when Uncle Carpus told me what he wanted me to do. But I just reminded myself that God had led me there, and so I did what needed to be done. I trust God and so I obeyed."

"Obedience to God should not depend upon our circumstances," Eunice said. "Our obedience is a result of our faith in God. If we trust God, then we can obey Him even when we don't understand what He is doing. God rewarded the obedience that Joshua and Israel showed at Jericho when He brought the walls down. I believe God will reward you the same. We don't have walls that need to come down, but God will meet your every need. I'm proud of you, Timothy. You have a good attitude in all of this.

"Now, who's hungry?" Eunice asked as she held a heaping plate toward Timothy.

"Oh, I am," Timothy replied as he took the plate.

"He's still a rascal," Lois said as she smiled softly.

Chapter 14

Doubt

The next day, Timothy went to the spice shop ready for anything. But instead of physical labor in the stables, Uncle Carpus kept Timothy's mind busy in the shop, quizzing him on both mathematics and the Jewish law. After several hours had passed, Carpus finally relented.

"Every Jewish boy ought to learn mathematics right alongside the law. Your mother and grandmother have taught you well the law of Moses. Did they teach you mathematics as well?"

"No, my father taught me mathematics and letters," Timothy replied.

"Good man, your father. Good teacher as well. You have an excellent understanding of both numbers and the law of Moses. Still, you have some odd notions about the Greeks, and by all rights, you need to be circumcised. I suppose that can be excused by your Greek father, though. Heaven knows, nobody around here would understand anything about that. And you must learn to speak up. If you know the answer, just say it. Don't let me drone on all day. My wife tells me I talk too much, but you don't think that. Anyway, I suppose all that's left to teach you now are the spices. We'll start here on the counter because these are the ones I sell the most. You'll need to remember their names and their uses, their smells, and their tastes, but most importantly, their prices. Heaven forbid that I leave you in here to mind the shop some day and you forget the prices. No, that won't do. You must pay close attention. Come over here, my boy."

Timothy moved closer to the counter and tried his best to pay attention to all the different spices. Some were easy to remember because they were familiar, but many of them Timothy had never seen or used before. Some of them Carpus gave to Timothy to taste, others he smelled. Carpus rambled on about how each one was processed and where it came from. Many of the spices Carpus bought in Iconium, but they originated in lands much further. Carpus grew some of the spices himself. These Timothy had seen yesterday in the fields. Occasionally, a customer broke the monotony of the lessons. When Carpus had finished naming and describing all the spices in the shop, he began to test Timothy on them. This time, Timothy did not fare as well as he had before.

"No, no, no," Carpus stopped Timothy, "nutmeg comes from the seed, mace comes from the outer covering of the seed. I think I have some in the back." Carpus disappeared into the back room and returned with several nutmeg seeds in his hand. "Look here," he said as he extended his hand toward Timothy. Timothy took one in his hand. He tried to feign interest, but his mind could no longer focus. Carpus saw the look on Timothy's face. "My dear boy! I've given you too much to remember all in one day. Lessons are over." Timothy dropped the nutmeg seed back into Carpus' hand. He was grateful for the break. He was a bit overwhelmed trying to remember all the different spices and everything about them. "Sweep the floors, then if you'll tend to Claudius for me, you'll be done for the day," Carpus smiled. "We'll begin again tomorrow morning."

Timothy quickly swept both the front and back rooms, then saw to Claudius. He rushed back to the shop, grabbed his pack, and headed for home. As Timothy walked home, he tried to remember all that Uncle Carpus had said, but it felt like grains of sand slipping through his fingers. He knew there was no way he could remember all that Carpus had taught him. Why had he convinced himself that he could do this job? It would be better if he just quit. Uncle Carpus could find someone else, someone who enjoyed spices as much as he did. When he arrived at home, Vitas, Rhea, and Horace were inside.

"Well, there you are!" Vitas greeted Timothy. Vitas and Horace were sitting together by the window near Lois. "Your grandmother was just telling us that you've been working in the market. I'd wondered what happened when you didn't come by yesterday."

"Tell the truth," Rhea interjected from across the room. She was by the fireplace with Eunice kneading bread together. "You were lonely trying to finish the room without him. Nobody to talk to all day long except a cripple and a woman." Rhea smiled as she teased her husband.

"It wasn't that bad, my dear," Vitas replied. Then with a smile, "Horace here is good company."

"Oh, you're awful," Rhea gasped in mock horror. Then turning to Timothy, "So, how do you like the life of a merchant?"

"Oh, I'm no merchant. I mean, I don't mind the work, but I don't know how Uncle Carpus keeps all the spices straight," Timothy replied. "My brain is about to explode. All day long, Uncle Carpus has been teaching me. At first, it was easy, things I already knew like mathematics and the Jewish law, but then he began on the spices. Cinnamon and cardamom, thyme and dill, basil and silphium. There's no way I can remember all their names, much less how to use them. I'm going to quit. Uncle Carpus is going to have to find someone else to help him."

"Now," said Eunice, "is it really that bad? Yesterday you were so happy to be there."

"Yesterday I didn't have to know the taste, smell, cost, and use of a hundred different spices. There's no way I can do this. I don't know what to do." Timothy collapsed onto one of the cushions by the fireplace. "I want to do this, but I'm not sure I can."

"That's right," Lois chimed in from across the room. "You can't do this. You shouldn't even try."

"*Immah*," Eunice began to scold her mother, "you said you would stay out of this."

"You should go ahead and quit," Lois continued as if she hadn't even heard her daughter. "After all, who are you? Just some poor widow woman's son who doesn't know parsley from pepper."

"Hey, I know pepper!" Timothy interjected.

"You sound exactly like Gideon when God sent his angel with a message," Lois replied.

"Oh! Who's Gideon?" Vitas asked excitedly at the possibility of a new story. "Nobody's told us about Gideon."

"Today's your day then," answered Lois. "Gather round and listen up. That means you, Timothy. After God brought His people out of Egypt and into the promised land, the people had rest. But only for a time. They began to follow the gods of the people that lived in the land. They worshipped the false gods and so God removed His favor from them. He allowed their enemies to rule over them. Israel was once again in bondage, this time in their own land. This happened many times over many years, but each time God sent a judge to rule over the land and to free the people from their bondage. These judges were to turn the hearts of the people back to God. One of these judges was Gideon."

"Gideon must have been a great man for God to choose him," stated Vitas.

"Oh, but he wasn't," Lois replied. "When the Lord sent his angel to tell Gideon what to do, Gideon responded that his clan was the weakest in all Israel and that he was the youngest of all his father's house. Gideon claimed that he was a nobody from a nobody family and that there must be some mistake. He was so unsure of himself that he tested God three times just to be sure that God knew what He was doing. The first time God consumed Gideon's offering with fire out of a rock. The second time God made dew to settle only on Gideon's fleece with the ground dry around it. The third time God made the dew settle on the ground, but not on Gideon's fleece.

"But that's not all. Gideon finally did lead an army to fight their enemies. He called the tribes to send men to fight. When the army gathered, there were 32,000 men. God told Gideon to allow all those who were afraid to return to their homes. Twenty-two thousand men were afraid and left. Only 10,000 brave men remained. Yet God told Gideon that the army was still too large. In the end, God sent Gideon to war with only 300 men. Gideon armed those men with ram's horn trumpets, empty jars, and torches within the jars."

"What happened next?" Vitas asked.

"Yes, what happened next?" added Horace.

"The men went to the edge of the enemy camp in the middle of the night," Timothy responded as he moved closer. "They smashed the jars and blew the trumpets. They raised the torches in the air and shouted, 'A sword for the Lord and for Gideon.' And God turned the swords of their enemies against each other. They fled from before Israel."

"Wow," Vitas responded in a hushed tone.

"So, God sent Gideon to war with only 300 men so that people would know that He had delivered them. Is that right?" Horace said a moment later. "God chose Gideon from a nobody family and sent a tiny army to face their enemies, so that everyone would know that God gave them the victory."

"Yes, exactly," Lois replied. "God received the praise for the victory, not Gideon. Sometimes God chooses to use weak vessels for the sole purpose of showing how powerful He is. Gideon knew that he was weak, but he failed to realize that his weakness was the precise quality that made him worth using. It's in our weakness that God can show Himself strong."

"So, you don't think I should quit," Timothy asked, more as a statement than a question.

"I can't believe I'm saying this," Lois answered, "but, no. I don't think you should quit. Don't quit just because you don't think you can do it. Knowing that you can't do something is the first step to allowing God to work through you. You believe God led you to do this?"

"Yes," Timothy answered.

"Then continue in this path until God leads you to the next path. Don't quit because it's hard," Lois replied.

"That's good advice," Rhea added, "for Timothy, but for the rest of us also. I've been thinking about this baby. I'm scared about what might happen when the baby comes. But this helps. Sometimes I feel so weak. How will I give birth to this child? How can I be a mother? But now I know God will help me through it. He'll help me and I'll praise Him every step along the way."

"Dear, you don't have a thing to worry about," Eunice comforted. "My mother and I will be there to help you when the child comes. I know God is going to bless you and the child as well. You'll be a terrific mother."

"And you'll be a terrific uncle," Timothy said to Horace.

"Hey! What about me?" Vitas exclaimed.

"I'm sure you'll be a terrific father too," laughed Timothy.

Chapter 15

Potential

Timothy and Horace continued to joke and laugh while Eunice and Rhea finished the meal preparations. Eunice was teaching Rhea some of her tricks for making bread.

"Your bread is always so good," Rhea said. "You have to show me how you make it."

"It's all in the way you knead it," Eunice replied. "Knead it too much and the crust will be too hard. Too little and the leaven won't mix thoroughly. It should be elastic and springy when you let it set."

"Yes, but how do you get it to look like that?" Rhea asked. "How do you twist it all together?"

"The *challah* bread?" Eunice asked. "It's not twisted, more like braided. You should come back tomorrow. We can make bread together and I'll show you how to prepare for the Sabbath meal."

"Really?" exclaimed Rhea. "Could you? We tried to keep the Sabbath last week, but I'm afraid we did it all wrong."

"All of you should come and spend the Sabbath with us this week," Eunice responded. "Timothy has taught you enough that you understand its importance and you've shown that you have a respect for and faith in God. You can come in the morning and I'll show you how we prepare all the meals. The men can come later, just before sunset when we begin."

"Sounds wonderful," Rhea replied.

"Did I hear someone talking about food?" Vitas asked as he came closer to the fire.

"It's not ready, not yet," Rhea said as she slapped his hand away from the food cooking on the fire. "But yes, we were talking about food. Eunice has invited all of us to take the Sabbath with them tomorrow."

"That's great! We can see how it's really done," Vitas replied. He reached for the buns that Eunice was pulling from the oven. Again, Rhea slapped at his hand.

"Shoo!" Rhea said with a smile.

"Actually, I think we're ready," Eunice responded. "Timothy, if you'll show Vitas where to wash, we're almost ready to eat."

"Come on," Timothy called to Vitas. "Let me show you how to get out of their way," he teased.

After they had finished their meal, Horace asked Lois, "Earlier when you were talking about Gideon, you said that Israel followed after false gods many separate times. Why would they do that?"

"For the same reason people do today, I imagine," Lois replied. "They forget to praise God for the blessings that He brings. Soon enough they credit themselves for their own success and forget about the God of heaven. Then they fall into difficulties and seek a god to help them. They see the false gods their neighbors follow, so they do as well. Every time Israel failed to follow God, He allowed their neighbors to rule over them."

"But then He sent judges, like Gideon, to lead them back to Him, right?" Vitas questioned.

"Were they all like Gideon?" Horace asked. "Men from nobody families that God used to show His power?"

"Some were. There was even one that was a woman: Deborah," Lois answered.

"Oh, a woman, I like her already," Rhea stated.

"I do too," Lois replied with a smile. "But not all of the judges were the same. One of them was very nearly the opposite of Gideon. His name was Samson. God sent an angel to announce his birth. Twice the angel came to speak to Samson's parents. The angel told them that their child would be holy to the Lord from before his birth. His mother was not to drink any wine or strong drink, nor could she eat of any unclean thing. After his birth, he must follow the same rules regarding unclean things. Neither were they to cut his hair. The child was to be holy, separated unto the Lord."

"Yeah, that doesn't sound anything like Gideon," Vitas proclaimed. "I can't imagine what God did with a man like that."

"If you'll be quiet," Rhea teased, "she might just tell us."

"When Samson was grown," Lois continued, "God gave him extraordinary strength. He killed a lion with his bare hands. He slew countless Philistines, the enemies of God's people. When his enemies captured him, he broke the ropes that bound him as if they were nothing. When they trapped him inside a city, he took the city gates and carried them away."

"I told you it'd be good," Vitas said proudly. "We should name our child Samson if he's a boy. Rhea, do you like the name Samson?"

"Not so fast," Lois answered. "Just because God gave Samson great strength, does not mean he was a great judge, or worthy namesake for your child."

"What do you mean?" asked Vitas. The confusion was clear on his face.

"God demanded that Samson live a life separated unto Him. Yet we know Samson not for his dedication to God, but for the compromises Samson made with the world."

"Oh no," Horace said. "What did he do?"

"Samson lusted after the desires of the flesh. His lust and pride cost him dearly. He believed himself to be better than other men. He lusted after Philistine women, though they served false gods. He married one and he loved another. The marriage didn't last as the Philistines betrayed him, but the one he loved, Delilah, cost him much more. The Philistines offered her enormous amounts of silver if she would discover the source of Samson's strength. After much begging and pleading, she finally found the truth. Samson told her that he was separated unto God and that if his hair was cut, his extraordinary strength would leave him."

"And she cut it, didn't she?" Vitas exclaimed in disgust.

"Yes," replied Lois. "The Philistines gave her the silver they had promised, and she betrayed him. When he was asleep, she called a servant to cut his hair. When he awoke, the Philistines captured him. They took Samson and gouged out his eyes. They bound him and made him grind grain in prison. One day, the Philistines held a great feast for their god. They brought Samson, so they could mock him and his God. At this feast in the temple of their false god, Samson stood between the main pillars of the structure. He prayed and asked God for one last measure of power that he might avenge the loss of his eyes. God gave him that last bit of strength and Samson tore down the pillars and the temple collapsed, killing all that were there. So, on the day of Samson's death, he killed more Philistines than he had in his life."

"Wow," Rhea said. "That's such a sad story. God had given him such great power, but he wasted it. He could have done so much more."

"Yes," Lois replied, "he could have. But he allowed his love for Delilah to come before his love for God."

"It's not his fault that the woman betrayed him," Vitas answered a bit defiantly.

"No, it's not," Timothy stated. "But it was his fault that he loved her more than he loved God. Delilah loved money more than she loved Samson. She served a false god, not his God. This was no secret. He knew who she was. She did what any Philistine would have done. Samson forgot that the source of his power was God, so God took the power. Samson gave to Delilah what he should have given to God–his trust."

"That's it," declared Vitas, "I'm never cutting my hair again."

"I don't think that's the point of the story, dear," Rhea answered.

"I know, but just to be safe," Vitas responded with both hands covering his head like a protective shield. "No, I get it," he said a moment later. "We must trust God and that means that nothing else comes before Him. That was the point that Samson missed. His strength and Delilah were more important to him than God. And he lost both of them."

"I think it would be better to be like Gideon than like Samson," Horace added. "Better to be a nobody who has a tough time trusting God but obeys, than to be a powerful somebody who trusts the wrong person and fails. To trust God means to obey. Even when you're not sure of yourself, you can be sure of God."

"I couldn't have said it better myself," Lois replied. "Neither Gideon nor Samson were perfect men, but while each one had their struggles, their obedience showed their faith or lack thereof. Our obedience shows our faith the same."

A momentary silence came upon the room. Then Rhea said, "I need to get this baby to bed." She gently patted her belly. "I'm exhausted. Vitas, help me up." Vitas jumped to his feet. He helped Rhea up from her position on the floor. She was starting to get much slower as her belly grew bigger. There were still several weeks before the baby should come, but Vitas had already begun to take extra care to help Rhea when she was getting up off the floor.

"We'll see you tomorrow morning," Eunice said to Rhea as they left.

"Is there anything I should bring?" Rhea asked.

"Some of that delicious cheese if you have some," Lois answered.

"I can do that," replied Rhea. "We'll see you tomorrow."

Chapter 16

The Difference

When Timothy arrived at the spice shop the next morning, he found Uncle Carpus in the back room sorting through spice chests and sacks. Normally in good order, the room was a mess. Uncle Carpus looked up from behind a large barrel, "Good, my boy, you're here. Take these sacks for me." Carpus handed Timothy several cloth sacks.

"What's going on?" Timothy questioned. "Is something wrong?"

"Oh no, my boy," replied Carpus, not looking up from the small wooden box he was holding. He reached into the box and sifted out a handful of a dull brown spice that Timothy felt like he should have recognized but didn't. Carpus dropped the spice back into the box, then looked up at Timothy. "No, there's nothing wrong. I'm only taking a quick inventory before we leave to go to Iconium."

"We're going to Iconium? Today?" Timothy blurted out.

"No, my boy. The Sabbath begins this evening. You know that. There's no way we could get there before sundown. It's too late in the day already. Anyway, there's too much to do before we go. We'll prepare everything for our journey today, then we'll leave the morning after the Sabbath. Take those sacks and the ones in that crate over there and put them in the cart. See to Claudius while you're back there, then I'll need your help up here again."

Timothy spent the rest of the morning carrying items back and forth to the cart. Many of the sacks were nearly empty and Carpus directed Timothy to empty these into the appropriate jars in the front room. Carpus watched as Timothy found the correct jars for each spice. Only twice did Carpus stop Timothy and direct him to a different jar. Carpus was almost pleased that Timothy had remembered so many spices. "Much better. We'll keep working on them until you remember all of them," he said. At noon Carpus dismissed Timothy, "I can finish all that is left. Go home and help your mother prepare for the Sabbath. Make sure she has all she needs for the next several days. Tell her we'll return the third or fourth day." As Timothy turned to go, Carpus called after him, "I want to leave well before sunrise, so be here early and ready to go."

"I will be," replied Timothy as he stepped out the door.

"And Timothy," Carpus called again, but this time his voice softened. "May you have a peaceful Sabbath, my son."

Timothy smiled. "And a peaceful Sabbath to you as well, my uncle," he replied. He turned back and gave the old man a hug. Timothy shook his head as he left. The old man might be a demanding boss, but he still cared for Timothy. He raced home eager to share the news of his upcoming journey. When he arrived, his mother, grandmother, and Rhea were all gathered around the fireplace laughing.

"What's so funny?" Timothy was curious.

"Oh, we're just telling stories about babies and all the wonderful things they do," his mother replied.

"Not again," Timothy buried his head in his hands. "Which story did you tell now?"

"All of them," Lois replied with a grin.

"Funny, funny. Anyway, guess what happened today," Timothy said, hoping to permanently change the subject. "I'm going with Uncle Carpus to Iconium!"

"Well now," Lois remarked, "look who likes working at the spice shop today."

"Sounds like an adventure," Rhea added.

"When do you leave?" Eunice asked.

"We leave after the Sabbath, early the next morning," Timothy replied. "Uncle Carpus said that we'll be gone three or four days. One day there, one day back, and two days to explore the city. I'm sure he'll take me to the market with him. I hope we go to the synagogue to pray also."

"He better take you to pray at the synagogue," Lois replied. "I want you to greet each of the rabbis when you are there and tell me all they have to say when you come back."

"Yes, *Sabta*," Timothy replied. "*Immah*, is there anything you need me to do for you now before I leave?"

"No," Eunice responded, "just pack your nice clothes to wear when you arrive in Iconium. Not for travel, but to wear while you're there. You can use my larger pack if they don't fit in yours. When you finish, find Vitas and Horace. Since you're home, they might as well come over too."

Timothy quickly packed his best clothes into the larger pack that his mother had offered. The clothes weren't any different than the ones he was wearing, they were just newer, and the color of the fabric had not yet faded. He shoved two knee-length tunics in the bag along with one pair of trousers in case it was cold. He placed another tunic beside his bed along with a cloak that he would wear on the journey. He set aside two waterskins to fill with fresh water before he left. This finished, he left to find Vitas and Horace. When he arrived at their home, he found the two men in the middle of a discussion.

"Wouldn't you want a king though?" Vitas insisted. "If they had a king, then their enemies wouldn't have been able to conquer them so easily."

"But if they had obeyed God, then they wouldn't have been conquered at all," countered Horace.

"Timothy!" Vitas spotted Timothy as he entered the courtyard. "Come settle this argument. Horace says that Israel should have listened to the judges and obeyed God. I agree that Israel should have obeyed God, but I say they would have been better off with a king. A strong king with an army would have kept their enemies away. What do you say?"

"I said," Horace interjected, "that having a king wouldn't make a difference if Israel still disobeyed God. Tell him everything, not just your side."

Vitas glared at Horace and Horace glared back. Then Vitas burst out in a great laugh. Horace began to smile as well. Then Vitas said, "You're right. You did say that. I think you're wrong, but I wasn't being fair."

"Thank you. That was kind. You're still wrong, though," Horace answered.

They both turned to Timothy, then Vitas asked, "So, what do you say? King? No king? Judges? What's the right answer?"

Timothy looked at them, thought for a moment, then said with a smile, "My mother said you can come over to our house anytime."

"Oh, come on!" Horace said. "Just give us an answer, so this big oaf can see the truth."

"Hey," Vitas feigned insult, "I thought we were being kind?"

"No," answered Horace mischievously, "you were being kind, I was being right."

"Come on, Timothy, what do you say?" Vitas prodded.

"Honestly, I think you're both right," Timothy answered. "Looking at it practically, a king would deter others from conquering Israel. But if Israel had obeyed God, then He would have protected them with or without a king. And even more, if there was a godly king, then he could lead the people to follow God in a greater way than a judge could."

"Ha!" shouted Vitas. "I knew a king would be better."

"But," continued Timothy, "a wicked king could lead Israel even further away from God."

"Ha!" Horace proclaimed triumphantly.

"After all," Timothy said, "Israel's history shows this to be true."

"Really, how?" asked Vitas. "Did Israel have a king?"

"Israel had many kings, but shouldn't we go back to my place so Rhea can hear the story as well?" Timothy said.

"Yeah, you're right. Let's go," Vitas said as he picked up Horace. "Lead the way."

When they arrived at Timothy's home, the three men settled down to continue their discussion. After rehashing the earlier discussion for the benefit of the women, Timothy continued. "The people wanted to be like all the other nations. They wanted to have a king. So, they asked the last judge, a godly man named Samuel, to give them a king. Samuel was distraught because he knew that the people would rather follow a person than to follow God. God told Samuel to warn the people of the dangers of having a king, and he did so. He told Israel that a king would lead them to war and take their sons and daughters to serve him. They would cry out to God because of the king, but on that day the Lord would not hear them. After Samuel told all this to the people, they still demanded a king.

"So, God gave them a king, a man named Saul. He was the tallest, strongest, best looking of all the men in Israel," Timothy said.

"Sounds nice," said Rhea.

"Yes," Vitas added sticking out his chest, "a man just like me."

"Samuel anointed Saul king of Israel and the people rejoiced that they had a king," Timothy continued. "But the day came when Saul disobeyed God. When told by God to destroy an enemy completely, he spared many of the animals and the enemy king. God was displeased by his disobedience in this and in other things, so God took the kingdom from him. God told Samuel to anoint a new king, a young man, about the same age as me. He was a shepherd, the youngest of eight brothers. His name was David."

"This sounds just like Gideon and Samson," Horace said. "Gideon and David were both the youngest sons, while Samson and Saul were both the biggest and strongest. Samson and Saul both failed to obey. Did David obey God like Gideon did?"

"David wasn't perfect; he made many mistakes. But he followed God with his whole heart," Timothy answered. "The difference between David and Saul was best seen during the greatest battle of their day. The Philistines had come to war against Israel while Saul was king. Each camp was at the base of a mountain with a valley between them. The Philistines had a giant in their camp. Each day he would come out into the valley and challenge the Israelites to single combat. He defiled the name of our God, yet no one from Israel would fight him."

"Saul should have fought him," Vitas stated. "If he was the biggest and strongest, he should have gone to face the giant."

"But he didn't, did he?" asked Horace.

"No, he didn't," Timothy replied. "David wasn't even in the army at that time. He was at home tending the sheep when his father sent him to take provisions to his older brothers who were in Saul's army. When David arrived at the camp and heard the blasphemy of the Philistine, he volunteered to fight him. Men brought him before King Saul. David told the king that God had delivered him from both a bear and a lion while protecting his father's sheep and that God would deliver him from this giant also. Saul sent David to battle against the giant. David rejected the king's armor but took a slingshot to battle instead."

"He didn't," Vitas said.

"He did. Armed only with a slingshot and a staff against the greatest warrior in the Philistine army, David went to war. But he didn't go alone. Before both armies, David declared that God would deliver the giant into his hand. He ran toward the giant and slung a stone that sank into the giant's forehead. The giant fell to the ground and David took the giant's own sword to cut off his head."

"That's incredible," Vitas exclaimed. "Did they make David king then?"

"No, not for many years, not until after Saul died," Timothy answered. "The two men became rivals and Saul tried to kill David many times, but God delivered him each time. But after Saul died, David became king."

"So, Saul took Israel to war," Horace said, "but couldn't deliver victory. David found Israel at war and turned to God for the victory."

"Precisely," Timothy replied.

Chapter 17

Decision

The afternoon passed quickly. Eunice and Rhea finished the meal preparations. Eunice carefully showed Rhea how to weave the bread while Lois and Timothy reviewed the Sabbath prayers with Vitas and Horace. Just before sunset, Timothy set out the Sabbath candles. Eunice and Lois normally lit the candles together, but Lois called Rhea over to take her place. Together Eunice and Rhea lit the candles. They all said the prayers together to welcome the Sabbath, then Eunice, Timothy, and Lois began to sing. The six friends gathered around the low table and began eating.

"Is it okay if we talk during the meal?" Rhea asked after a moment of silence.

"Yes," Eunice replied, "the Sabbath is a day to rejoice and praise the Lord for all his blessings. We do not talk of business or worldly matters, but we do talk."

"Usually," Timothy added, "we sing. There are so many songs of praise that we can teach you. But *Immah* should do that. She knows all the songs, in Greek and in our local tongue. My father helped her to translate some of them, so we could sing them together."

"Would you sing for us?" Rhea asked Eunice.

Eunice looked around the room, then closed her eyes and began to sing, "I will exalt you, my God and my King. I will bless your name forever. Every day I will bless your name forever." As she continued singing, Timothy and Lois joined her. Together they sang their praise to the Lord. When they had finished, Rhea demanded more. They continued singing until their voices began to tire.

Lois said, "We can sing more tomorrow. This is a day of rest and it is time that we do exactly that."

"Your singing is so beautiful," Rhea said. "My father had a lyre that he would play when I was little. These songs make me feel as if God is right here with us."

"Tomorrow we can teach you some of the songs," Eunice said. "Come back then, and we can go over some of the easier ones."

"I'd love that," Rhea replied.

*

The sun was already high above the horizon, but Timothy had not yet left his bed. He was awake, but still lying on his mattress thinking about the adventure that would begin the next day. He had not been to Iconium since before his father had died. He wondered at the changes he would find. He could hear his mother and grandmother in the courtyard. He could picture them in their chairs. They were talking, but Timothy could not make out the words. When he heard his name several times, he finally rolled out of his bed and went to welcome the day.

"So, I heard you two talking about me," he said with a smile. "Anything I should know?"

"Oh no," replied Lois. "We were just wondering how long my grandson was going to sleep today."

"He may have slept longer," Timothy answered, "but the sun woke him up long ago."

"Then," Eunice asked, "why didn't you come out here with us?"

"I was just thinking about the journey tomorrow."

"Are you nervous?" Eunice prodded. "It's been a long time since you have gone that far from home."

"No," Timothy answered, "I'm not nervous. Excited, I think. I feel like this is a whole new step for me. I decided to follow the path of God, and he has blessed me with a job and new friends. I wonder what new things I might find on this journey."

"You're going to be fine," Lois said. "Yes, God is going to use you."

Just then the gate opened, and Vitas came in with Horace. "A peaceful Sabbath to you," Vitas greeted. He placed Horace on the ground near Lois.

"Where's Rhea? You didn't leave her behind, did you?" Lois scolded.

"No, no, she's coming," he answered. "She just moves a bit slower right now. I'm going to help her." Vitas headed back for the gate, but narrowly missed being hit as Rhea swung the gate open and stepped inside.

"I think I'm ready for this baby to come," she said as Vitas danced past the gate and gave her his arm. "I can't even walk from our house to yours without having to rest a bit." She sat down on a stool right inside the gate. "The sun seems awfully warm for this time of day. Is anybody else hot?"

"Oh, my dear," Eunice said, "you need to come inside where it's cooler. Timothy, bring a pitcher of water for her to drink." Timothy jumped to bring the water and Vitas helped Rhea move inside. Once she was situated, Timothy gave her the water. She drank deeply.

"Thank you," Rhea said, "I feel much better now. I can't get comfortable at night and I can't sleep. I'm just tired all the time. Does it get better?"

"In about another month," Lois responded.

"But then you'll have a whole new kind of tired," Eunice smiled.

"Something to look forward to," Rhea replied. "Would you sing again? I'd like to just listen for a while if that's okay." Rhea leaned back into the cushion while Eunice and Lois sang. Vitas checked to make sure she was comfortable, then he and Timothy went back out to the courtyard and sat next to Horace.

"Is she okay?" Horace asked.

"I think so," Vitas answered. "I hope so. I don't know, I've never done this before. What do I know about pregnant women?"

"My mother and grandmother will take care of her," Timothy said. "They would have told us if there was something to be worried about."

The three friends sat in the courtyard and returned to their discussion of the day before. Horace wanted to know all about the kings of Israel. He wanted to know which had followed God, which had not. Vitas was more interested in the wars they had fought. Timothy described the division of Israel into two nations, Israel and Judah. He told of all the kings he could remember. As he began to rehearse the evils of Ahab and Jezebel, his mother came out to the courtyard.

"If the men care to join us, it's time for the noon meal."

"Wonderful," Vitas declared with a smile. "I believe we will join you." Then he asked in a lower tone, "Is Rhea okay?"

"She's fine," Eunice answered. "I dare say that she may deliver the baby sooner than expected, but all of this is as it should be. She's young and stronger than you think." Vitas nodded appreciatively and whispered his thanks. Then he took

Horace in his arms, and they all moved inside. They had just begun their prayers when a call came from the courtyard.

"A peaceful Sabbath to all that dwell within this house!" The voice was familiar. Uncle Carpus had come to take the meal with them. Timothy rushed outside. Carpus and his wife, Hannah, were both standing in the courtyard.

"A peaceful Sabbath to both of you," Timothy greeted each of them. "You must come in. We have just begun to eat. Join us."

"Thank you, my son," Carpus responded. "We had hoped to share the Sabbath with you, your mother, and your grandmother. There are far too few of us in Lystra to spend the Sabbath alone." The three of them went inside. "You have guests. We didn't know. We will leave," Carpus stated stiffly as soon as he saw the three strangers at the table.

"No, Uncle," Timothy replied, "these are God-fearers. This is Vitas and his wife Rhea. Horace is their cousin. They have rejected the pagan gods and choose to follow the God of heaven. They have joined us for the Sabbath so that they may learn to respect the ways of God."

Vitas stood to his feet, "A peaceful Sabbath to you, my friend. The God of the Jews is the one true God. My friend Timothy has taught us of your God. My house has forsaken the gods of our people, and we fear none but the God of heaven."

"A peaceful Sabbath to you," Carpus said, if a bit stiffly. He relaxed only a bit as he took a place next to Timothy.

"Come, Hannah, sit with me," Lois called. "It is so good to see you."

"It's good to see you also," Hannah replied as she moved to take a place next to Lois. "Thank you for sharing your table with us." Hannah greeted Eunice the same, then turned to Rhea. Her eyes were kind and gentle. She spoke softly, yet clearly, "Children are a gift from the Lord, and the fruit of the womb is a reward." Then she reached for Rhea's hand. As she took her hand she prayed, "The Lord bless you and keep you. The Lord make His face to shine upon you and be gracious unto you. The Lord lift His countenance upon you and give you peace."

"That was beautiful," said Rhea. "Is that from the songs?"

"The first part about children, yes," Hannah replied. "The rest was the blessing Moses told his brother to give to the people."

"You're truly kind. Thank you," Rhea said.

They finished the meal in silence as Carpus eyed Vitas and his family with caution. For Timothy, this was completely unorthodox as he had never heard Uncle Carpus go more than a minute without prattling on about some event or detail that had once happened. Vitas once tried to break the silence by asking how long Carpus had lived in Lystra. Carpus had grunted an unintelligible answer and returned silently to his meal. When the meal was completed, Carpus gave a quick prayer of thanksgiving for the hospitality and walked out into the courtyard. Hannah followed him, but first she saluted Rhea, Vitas, and Horace, "The peace of God be upon you all."

Carpus had already left by the time Timothy and Lois made it to the courtyard with Hannah. Hannah, however, stopped to apologize for their brief stay. "I'm afraid living here among Greeks all these years has done nothing to change my husband's ideas about proselytizing. He feels that the God of heaven is for the Hebrews and that the heathen nations deserve nothing but God's wrath. I'm glad you do not. But I must go," Hannah stated. "Lois, you must visit me this week. My husband will be gone, and we have much to talk about."

"I believe I may," Lois said. The two women embraced, then Hannah left to chase after her husband.

As Timothy came back inside, Vitas asked, "Is everything alright?"

"Yes, they simply returned home," Timothy answered. "They would not have come if they knew we already had guests. They did not want to intrude on you as our guests."

"Ah," Vitas replied. "He is the spice merchant, no? You can tell by his clothes. He carries himself like a rich man. We're probably just too poor for him to be around."

"I liked his wife," Rhea said. "She prayed for me and said my child is a gift from the Lord."

"I like his wife as well," Lois added. "She's one of my dearest friends. Him, on the other hand…"

"*Immah*!" Eunice stopped her mother.

"I was only going to say that, yes, he is the spice merchant," Lois replied.

"Sure you were," Timothy laughed. "*Sabta* doesn't like Uncle Carpus much. It's because he's got shifty eyes."

"You stop it!" Eunice smiled as she slapped Timothy on the shoulder. "This is not talk for the Sabbath!"

"You're right, *Immah*," Timothy answered. "We should probably go back to our talk about the kings and the prophets," he said to Vitas and Horace.

"Wait, who are the prophets?" asked Rhea.

"The prophets were the men that God sent to straighten out the kings when they messed up," Vitas answered. "Timothy was telling us about all the kings earlier while you were resting. Some of them were good, like David, but others were pretty bad." Then he turned to Timothy, "You were telling us about the evil king and queen that turned the people against God. What were their names again?"

"Jezebel and Ahab," Horace answered. "Ahab was the king, and Jezebel was the queen."

"Yes," Timothy continued. "Ahab and Jezebel made Israel sin before the Lord. Ahab did more to provoke the Lord to anger than all the kings who came before him. So, God raised up the prophet Elijah. Elijah told Ahab that there would be no rain because of his sin before the Lord. For three years there was no rain. The rivers dried up and famine spread across the land. Finally, Elijah came before Ahab and challenged him to a duel."

"Yes," Vitas cried. "Ahab's in trouble."

Timothy laughed. "Yes, but not how you're thinking. The duel was not to be between the king and Elijah, but between God and Ahab's false god Baal. The king called all the people to Mt. Carmel to witness the duel. Elijah told the people that they must choose which side they would serve. They could not serve both God and Baal. The 450 prophets of Baal stood to one side and Elijah stood by himself on the other. The challenge was this: both sides would build an altar. On the altar they would place wood and a sacrifice. But no one would light a fire. The god who consumed their offering with fire would be the true God.

"Elijah let the prophets of Baal go first. They built their altar with the wood and sacrifice. Then they began praying to their god. But he didn't answer. Then Elijah began to mock them. He said that their god must be sleeping or gone on a journey."

"That's great!" Vitas exclaimed. "That must have made them mad. What did they do?"

"Elijah's mocking only made them cry out to their god even more," Timothy replied. "They began to cut themselves, trying to gain their god's attention. All day long they cried out, but nothing happened.

"Then at the time of the evening sacrifice, Elijah repaired the altar of the Lord. He placed the wood and the sacrifice the same as the others had. Then he dug a trench around the altar. He called for water to be poured over the altar."

"Why would he do that?" Vitas asked in shock. "Water doesn't burn."

"Just listen," Rhea said. "Don't you want to find out?"

"Okay, I'll be quiet."

"Twelve barrels of water were poured over the altar until everything was soaked. The trench was filled with water. Then Elijah prayed. He asked God to show that He is the Lord. He prayed that the hearts of the people would be turned back to Him."

"And then?" Vitas asked.

"Shh!" Horace and Rhea both said.

"And then fire fell from heaven and consumed not only the sacrifice and the wood, but also the stones of the altar and the water in the trench."

"Yes!" shouted Vitas. "Fire from heaven! Wow."

"And did the people turn back to God?" Horace asked.

"For a time, yes they did," Lois replied. "That day they executed all of the prophets of Baal. But Ahab and Jezebel still ruled the land. Jezebel tried to kill Elijah, but God protected him. God showed him that he wasn't alone, there were still 7,000 men in Israel who had not bowed to Baal. Then he sent him to anoint a new king and call another prophet in his place. But the truth of Elijah's message still rings true today. There are those who would serve both God and Baal. Only they don't call their other god Baal, they call him Zeus, or time, or wealth, or pleasure, or health. But as Elijah said, we must choose who we will serve. People cannot serve two gods."

"And God in heaven showed He was God," Horace said.

"Is He still the same God today?" asked Rhea. "The God who hears us when we call and is pleased when we obey?"

"He is the same eternal God that made Abram a great nation, that guided Moses out of Egypt, who delivered David from the giant, and sent Elijah fire from heaven. He is the God that saves, that delivers, that provides and protects," Lois answered.

"My family chooses that God," Vitas said.

"As does mine," Timothy echoed.

Chapter 18

Darkness

Eunice shook Timothy gently. "Wake up, Timothy. It's time for you to leave." Timothy opened his eyes to darkness. He could make out the shape of his mother next to him. "Good morning, son. Carpus will be waiting."

Timothy sat up and rubbed his eyes. *Did his mother wake this early every morning?* he thought. "Good morning, *Immah*."

"Look at me," Eunice said softly. Timothy turned and stared intensely into the darkness. He could not make out the features of his mother's face in the dark. She took his hand and placed her pack into his hands. Timothy had packed it before the Sabbath. It was heavier now than he had left it. "I filled the waterskins, and there are hot buns inside. There is also a small bag of coins. It's not much, but if you need anything, your grandmother and I have given it to you."

"No, *Immah*," Timothy began to refuse the coins. He knew they did not have much. "You should keep the coins. What if you need something while I am gone?"

"If we need something," Eunice said, "God will provide. This is God's provision for you. Besides, you'll only be gone a few days." She closed both of Timothy's hands around the pack and began to pray, "We seek You, Lord, and You hear us. Deliver us from our fears. You make our faces to shine, and we are not ashamed. The poor cry out and You save us from our troubles. May the angel of the Lord camp around those who fear Him and deliver us."

"I love you, Timothy," Eunice whispered.

"I love you too, *Immah*."

Timothy quickly made his way to Carpus' house. He knocked at the gate. It was Hannah that answered, "Timothy?" she said as she peeked past the candlelight.

"Yes, ma'am," Timothy replied.

"Come in. Carpus is in the stables," she said.

Timothy slipped past her and headed for the stables. Carpus was busy preparing the harness for Claudius. "Good morning, Uncle," Timothy called.

"Timothy, my boy," Carpus answered. "Help me with the harness." Together they quickly fixed the harness on Claudius and attached it to the cart. Timothy added his own pack to the rest of the items that he had helped to stow. Most of the chests and sacks were empty, although there were a few chests of spices that Carpus grew that he was taking to sell in Iconium. Carpus said his goodbyes to Hannah, then he and Timothy left on their way.

Carpus led Claudius through the quiet streets of Lystra to the city gates. There was no room in the cart for passengers, it had not been designed for such anyway. This cart was for moving goods, not people. Timothy and Carpus would be walking just the same as Claudius. As they left the city behind, Timothy looked back. He imagined he could see his mother sitting by the fire. He hoped she had gone back to sleep for a while. He turned toward the path ahead.

It was not difficult to keep pace with Claudius. The donkey was not slow, but the pace at which Carpus had set him would be an easy pace to maintain for all three of them. In the quiet stillness of the dark morning, the only sounds were that of Claudius clomping down the road and the wheels of the cart against the stone pavement. It seemed as if the darkness demanded quiet. Timothy wondered if Carpus felt the same. He also wondered if Carpus was upset about the day before. Timothy had never considered that some Jews thought that God's blessings were for them alone. His own father had been Greek and had trusted the God of heaven. Timothy's mother and grandmother had encouraged his father to do so. Timothy thought of these things for the next hour until the sun rose above the horizon.

"Carpus," Timothy said as the light spilled across the sky, "are you upset that we were teaching Vitas and his family about the things of God?"

"My boy," Carpus replied, "it's more complicated than that. You're only doing what you have been taught. I lay no fault at your feet."

"But you think that the Greeks should be left to worship their false gods?" Timothy asked.

"I think that the pagans deserve the wrath of God for their idolatry," Carpus answered. "They are different than we are. They hold different morals than we do. They lie and steal. They care not for human life. They kill for the pleasure it brings. They seek after fleshly pleasures and worship the pursuit of these things. I wish God would destroy all those who worship false gods from the face of the earth. Then we would have peace."

"But you have lived here among them for so long. Don't you have sympathy for them? If they only knew God as we do, they would repent of their sins and turn from their ways," Timothy replied. "What of my father? He was a Greek. What about me?"

"My boy," Carpus said. He stopped in his path. "Your father converted to our faith that he might marry your mother. But many more are the examples of our people converting to false gods. Your father was the exception, not the rule. As for you, you have Jewish blood, however diluted it might be." Carpus began walking again. Timothy walked along in silence for a few moments.

"You said I should speak my mind when I know the answer," Timothy began now with a different tack. "Now, I must speak. God once told the prophet Jonah that he was to preach repentance to Nineveh. The people of Nineveh were enemies to our people. They were pagans that worshipped false gods. Yet God cared enough for them that He sent a prophet to teach them to repent. But Jonah ran from God so that he would not have to preach God's forgiveness to a people he hated.

"Jonah fled from the presence of God. He boarded a boat to sail away from Nineveh, but God did not let him escape. God sent a storm to slow Jonah in his flight. Yet Jonah was determined to run from God. He confessed to the sailors that the storm had come because he was running from God. Rather than return to Nineveh and preach repentance to his enemies, Jonah told the sailors to end his life by throwing him into the sea.

"But God was patient with the prophet and spared his life. God sent a great fish to swallow Jonah whole. Three days he remained in the belly of the fish, until God told it to spit Jonah on dry ground. Only then did Jonah go to Nineveh and preach repentance."

"Perhaps you should have been apprenticed to a rabbi, not a simple spice merchant," Carpus teased Timothy. "What are you trying to say, my boy?"

"The prophet was not a bad man because he hated the enemies of his people," Timothy replied. "Jonah loved God and loved his people. He wanted the blessings of God for him and his people. But he forgot that the God of heaven is not just the God of Abraham, Isaac, and Jacob. Before He was the God of Abraham, He was the God of Noah. He is the God who made Adam in the garden. God does not belong to just one tribe or nation. We belong to Him. He made us. All of us."

"But God's wrath must be poured out on the pagans," Carpus stopped Timothy. "All come from the same blood in Adam and Noah, you're right. But the pagans have forsaken the God that created them. For this, God must judge them. Surely you do not believe that God will just forgive all people's sins. There must be a penalty for sin. God taught this to Adam in the garden."

"That the pagans have turned their backs on God, there is no question," Timothy answered. "That is why God sent Jonah to Nineveh to preach repentance. People must turn from their sin. The pagans needed to understand that they had sinned against God, and He allowed them to repent of their sins. Isn't this the reason God called our people out from the nations? God called Abraham to be a blessing to all the families of the earth. God's blessing wasn't just for Abraham, nor was it for Jonah alone. God's forgiveness is a gift that He offers to all those who turn to Him. Don't the Scriptures say that we will be a light to all the nations that salvation may reach the ends of the earth?"

"Well," Carpus began, "I am no Jonah. I won't run from God if He calls me to go to Nineveh. I have lived among the Greeks all my life. I suppose I could live with Persians just the same. Did I tell you about the spices that come from Persia? They have excellent spices there. Saffron is the spice you must get from Persia. The Romans just love it. There was a troop of soldiers that came through a while back…"

Carpus continued talking, but Timothy knew the conversation was over, at least for now. Carpus rambled on about Persian spices, then about a Persian he once knew. Yet Timothy's mind remained fixed upon this idea of God bringing salvation to the ends of the earth. Would God send someone today to a place like Lystra just as He had sent Jonah to Nineveh? Would Lystra repent of their pagan gods like Nineveh had? Maybe Vitas and his family were just the beginning of the salvation God would bring to Lystra.

Chapter 19

Fruitful

A short while later, Carpus pointed out a small cluster of trees. "Let's stop over there for a moment." While the two men relieved themselves, Claudius munched on the grass that grew in abundance near the trees. "There must be an underground spring here," Carpus said. "Look how the grass and the trees are still green, while everything else around here is turning brown."

"Look," Timothy called from the other side of the trees, "there's a fig tree over here. I think they're ripe." Timothy plucked two of the purple fruits from the tree and handed one to Carpus.

"You're right, my boy," Carpus said as he broke open the fig. "See how the skin is soft and some of the nectar is coming out here. Look at that one. See how it's still green and stiff at the stem? If you try to eat that one, it'll be bitter. Not like these," Carpus said as he took a bite.

Timothy broke his open and took a bite as well. The taste of sweet honey filled his mouth. "Do we have time to gather more?" he asked Carpus.

"Let's take a few more, but just the ones that are ripe. Leave the others for the next travelers that pass," Carpus answered. Within minutes, they had carefully filled a small basket. "That should be enough. We can even share with my son and his family tonight." Timothy packed the basket into the cart and secured it enough so that it wouldn't be jostled.

As the two men continued their journey on the road, Carpus returned to the earlier conversation from that morning. Even though he had tried to move past what Timothy had said, he felt as if further explanation was in order. "My boy, I don't want you to think of your Uncle Carpus as a bad person. I know that we have a bit of difference in how we see things. I want you to know that I do believe in God and try to keep His law as best I can. Heaven knows that I'm not perfect, but I try to do what is right. I don't cheat those who come to purchase spices from me. I charge a fair price, from the rich the same as from the poor."

"Uncle," Timothy replied, "I don't think you are a bad person. I never meant to imply that. And I know that you are fair with all of your customers."

"Good," Carpus said. "Now as for the Greeks.... Are you familiar with the prophet Daniel?"

"The one that was taken to Babylon and made to serve in the palace of their king?" Timothy answered with a smile.

"Yes, that one," Carpus replied. "Your mother has taught you well the history of our people."

"Not just my mother, my grandmother as well," Timothy added.

"Ah, well, yes. Anyway," Carpus stammered, "Daniel and his friends were brought before the king and given the benefit of all the king's table. Food and wine to their heart's content. Yet Daniel rejected these and chose a diet of vegetables and water. Do you know why?" Timothy began to answer, but before he could, Carpus answered for himself. "Some say it was because the food had been offered to the pagan idols, and that may be true, but I think it was something else. Daniel had been taught, just like you, about all the foods that are clean and unclean according to God's law. The food that they were offered must have been from among the unclean foods and Daniel recognized that."

"But what about the wine?" Timothy asked. "Why did they reject the wine?"

"Because they were sons of Solomon, that's why," Carpus answered. "What did Solomon say to his son? 'Wine is a mocker, strong drink is raging, and whoever is deceived by it is not wise.' They knew the words of their father Solomon and took to heart the advice within them."

"I'd never thought about that," Timothy replied. "But what does any of this have to do with the Greeks?"

"Because just as Daniel lived among the Babylonians, we live among the Greeks," continued Carpus. "Daniel and his friends recognized the sins of those around them and kept themselves clean before God in heaven. He and his friends refused to defile themselves with the unclean things of the world around them. Sin will surround you whether you live in Babylon, Lystra, or even back home in Israel. They abstained from the things that would corrupt them but submitted to those things that were merely different. You see, my boy, there are things that people do that are different from our people, but that does not make them wrong. They submitted to the education given by the Babylonians but were wise enough to recognize the error of the pagan's ways. You must know in your heart and your mind that which is true, so that you will recognize lies as the falsehood they are. God blessed them, and they rose to high positions in the king's service because of this. They even allowed their captors to rename them. Just like me, yes, they were. They surrendered their Hebrew names and took Babylonian names."

"What do you mean?" Timothy asked. "You have a Babylonian name?"

"No," laughed Carpus, "I have a Greek name." He looked at Timothy and saw the confusion on his face. "You don't know? My boy, Carpus isn't the name my parents gave me. Carpus is the name your father gave me."

"Why? How? When? What do you mean?" Timothy stumbled to find the right words.

"Your father had just moved back to Lystra with your mother when we met. Actually, Hannah found your mother in the market first. Your mother had not yet learned the local language and was struggling to understand the vendors. Hannah helped her that day to find what she needed. We were thrilled to find another Jew this far from home. Anyway, your father came by my shop the next day with some goat cheese, to serve as thanks for my wife's help the day before. The shop was not so prosperous back then as it is now. I was a much skinnier man then, yes I was," Carpus reminisced while patting his belly.

"Your father and I spent the rest of the morning talking. I told him how the shop was struggling. He told me the reason no one came to my shop was because I was a foreigner. People didn't trust me. He said that if I wanted to show the locals that I was trustworthy, I should be more like them. He said I could at least take a name that was familiar."

"My father gave you the name Carpus?" Timothy was still in shock over this surprise revelation.

"You don't approve?" Carpus laughed. "Or do you think you have a better name? I've grown to like the name."

"But why did he pick Carpus?" Timothy asked. "But more than that, what's your real name? You have to tell me!"

"Oh, do I now?" Carpus was enjoying this moment of confusion from Timothy. "Okay, I'll tell you. Your father gave me the name Carpus because it has the same meaning as my Hebrew name, Ephraim. They both mean fruitful. And I took the name because I wanted my shop and family to be fruitful."

"Ephraim," Timothy said, "like the son of Joseph, the tribe of Israel?"

"That's the one, my boy," Carpus replied. "But listen to me now. Just as Daniel and his friends lived in a foreign land, so do we. Just as they kept themselves pure before God, so must we. Why do you think I tested you on the law of Moses? Because you will see and learn much in Lystra that is contrary to the law and you must know the difference. If you don't know what is right, how can you refuse that which is wrong? You must keep yourself pure before God regardless of what those around you do or say. This is the lesson of Daniel. The four Hebrew friends did not defile themselves and God blessed them because of their obedience."

"But what is the purpose of God's blessing?" Timothy asked. "That we might gather riches unto ourselves? That the pagans around us perish in their sins while we go free?" Timothy's mind raced with questions that appeared to have no answers. Even Uncle Carpus walked along in silence. Then Timothy continued, "I know that we must obey the law of God. This is how we show our faith in Him. But God's blessing is meant to draw people to Him. I know it is. God wants all people to come to Him."

"I don't know about that, my boy," Carpus interjected. "I say it is enough that we obey God's commands. If God wants to save the pagans, then He will do it. He doesn't need you or I to go about trying to convince them."

Timothy shook his head as they continued walking. "Ephraim," he whispered. Then with a sly smile on his face, "Can I call you Ephraim?"

"The only person that still calls me Ephraim is my dear Hannah," Carpus replied. "You may call me Uncle. That will do."

"Okay, Uncle Ephraim," Timothy laughed.

"You laugh it up," Carpus teased. "Maybe one of these days I'll tell you your real name."

"Wait!" Timothy said. "What do you mean my real name?"

Chapter 20

Dust

Carpus and Timothy continued toward Iconium as the sun rose higher into the sky. Carpus had begun to speak of all the things they would find in Iconium. For a while, Timothy paid close attention, but as Carpus began to ramble, he occupied himself by counting his steps. After twice reaching a thousand, he began to count Carpus' words. Timothy figured the old man spoke three times as fast as he walked. An hour had passed since Timothy last spoke, but Carpus had not stopped talking once in that time. However, neither one seemed bothered by the situation. While Carpus' speech did not falter, his pace had begun to slow. The sun was beating down upon them and even Timothy was ready for a break. When Carpus spotted a well, he directed Claudius toward it. The well was not new but looked to have been maintained. The wooden structure rose high into the air, three times taller than Timothy. At the top, a long wooden beam hung like a balance, one arm waving on either side of the structure. A lengthy rope attached to the narrow end of the beam while the heavier end served as a counterbalance. A bucket was tied to the other end of the rope. Below the bucket, a hole opened into the ground. The counterbalance provided by the wooden arm allowed a person to drop the empty bucket into the hole and pull a full bucket from the underground spring with little effort. Carpus sat in the shade of the cart and Timothy hurried to give the donkey water. After the donkey had drunk his fill, Timothy refilled all their waterskins and sat down next to Carpus.

"This well marks the halfway point between Lystra and Iconium," Carpus informed Timothy. Timothy handed the old man a fresh waterskin. "Thank you, my boy." After he drank from the waterskin, Carpus continued, "The Romans paved this road long before either of us was born. This well is the only reminder of the camp that once stood here. Now it serves old men like me who need a pause on their journey."

Timothy looked around. He could see the hills in the distance to the left. The terrain around him was dry and rocky, broken only by the dusty road on which they were traveling. He tried to imagine a Roman army camp, with tents and soldiers filling the emptiness.

"I once heard that the Romans were not the ones who built this road originally, but that it was the Persians," Carpus continued. "Maybe even the Persians of Daniel's day, but that was hundreds of years ago. Now, there're no signs that the Persians were even here. Just the Romans, infernal Romans everywhere you look."

Timothy took the buns out of his pack and handed one to Carpus. "One of these days, the Romans will be gone too. Nothing but dust, my boy, nothing but dust," Carpus closed his eyes as he leaned back against the wheel of the cart. "That's why you must be careful of the lies of their false gods. The Egyptians, the Babylonians, the Persians, the Greeks, now the Romans, all of them and their gods, they will all fade from history. Only one God remains. Only one God stands the test of time."

"Isn't that what Daniel's friends showed us?" Timothy asked.

“How do you mean?” Carpus replied, cracking one eye open to look at Timothy.

“When the Babylonian king built his idol and forced everyone to bow before it,” Timothy responded. “The king built an immense statue of himself and told everyone to bow before it and worship when the music played. Everyone bowed before the idol, except Shadrach, Meshach, and Abednego, Daniel’s friends that rejected the king’s food.”

“Okay, Rabbi,” Carpus teased Timothy. He opened both eyes and looked at Timothy. “I know the story. Let me ask you this, where was Daniel when his friends stood before the king?”

“I don’t know,” Timothy answered. Then with a smile, “He was probably here, building this road.”

“Ha!” laughed Carpus. “Okay, so tell me, what do we learn from the three Hebrew friends? Continue your story.”

“All I wanted to say is that they knew only one God would remain,” Timothy said. “They refused to bow before the idol because they believed in the one true God. Even when the king offered them a second chance to bow before the idol, they refused his offer. They could have bowed publicly and then continued worshipping God privately, but they refused to compromise. They told the king that they would not worship his idol. They said they wouldn't bow and, even if it cost them their lives, they would not worship the false god.”

“See, that’s what I’m talking about,” Carpus interrupted. “You have to be careful around these pagans. They’ll kill you just because you worship a different God than they do. It doesn’t matter that you are a person of faith, or that you have lived a good life. They’re completely without morals. The Babylonians saw the faith that these men had and still tried to kill them. They had no respect for them or their God. Just like the Romans today. Claudius would kill the Jews just for the fun of it.” At the sound of his name, Claudius let out a loud bray.

"Not you, my friend, I'm talking about your namesake in Rome," Carpus laughed.

"The king tried to kill them, but the fire did not consume Shadrach, Meshach, and Abednego," Timothy argued. "God delivered them in the midst of the fire and the Babylonian king even saw God walking around in the fire with them. The king saw God because Shadrach, Meshach, and Abednego remained firm in their conviction to serve only the true God in heaven. Their willingness to sacrifice their lives for their belief in God was the exact tool that God needed to reveal His power to the pagans.

"Too often we speak as if persecution is the worst thing that can happen," Timothy continued. "Be careful of the Romans, be careful of the Greeks. But some of the so-called persecution Israel faced was not persecution at all. It was the correction of a Father toward a rebellious son. Look at how many times Israel turned their back on God. That's why Israel was in Babylon to start with. They had rejected God and so He spread them like seeds before the wind. And when true persecution comes, as with the Hebrew friends, it is not God punishing His children for their faith but revealing Himself to the nations through their faith. We think God has forgotten about us if we face the smallest bit of opposition. I know I have. When my father died, I thought God had forgotten me. I thought the death of my father was the worst thing that could happen. But God used my father's death to strengthen my faith and now I have turned to follow Him with my whole heart."

Carpus began to interject, but Timothy pushed a step further, "You implied it yourself. The pagans will always be there to oppose us. It was Babylonians, then Persians, now Romans, but they're all the same. They were all great nations that served false gods and someday they will be nothing but dust. By our faithfulness to God, especially in the face of persecution, God can show His power to the pagans. The pagan gods will fall before the God of heaven. The Romans may kill us because we serve a different God than theirs. Well, I would gladly give my life if God would reveal Himself to the people of Lystra. I wish that all could see God as we see Him. God made us from dust and to dust we will return. I just want everything in between to matter," Timothy concluded.

"Now, Timothy," Carpus countered, "you must not get carried away in your zeal. I understand your excitement. I was a young man once also. But you must not seek out death. Death will come too quickly as it is. To proclaim your faith to the pagans is to court death. No, my boy, be content to live a quiet, consistent life in obedience to the law of God. Pray that God blesses you with a long life and a peaceful death."

"No," Timothy answered. "That is not what Shadrach, Meshach, and Abednego did. Their faith made them bold when they answered the king. I don't pray for death, but neither did they. I do admire that they did not fear death. They didn't value their lives so highly that they were willing to compromise their faith in God. I pray that God grants me the same grace to live my life with that kind of boldness. And if He deems that I must walk through the fire of faith so that He may reveal Himself to the nations, I pray only that many people see Him in the light of my life."

Silence stretched from the mountains to the opposite horizon. Timothy wondered if he had said too much. Finally, Claudius shook in his harness and stomped his hooves. "Yes, Claudius, it is time for us to be going," Carpus said. "Help me up, my boy." Timothy helped the old man to his feet.

Timothy stuffed their packs back into the cart. As he did, he spied the figs. He grabbed one and split it in half. Offering one half to Carpus, he said, "Something sweet for my favorite uncle."

Carpus glanced at the fruit then at Timothy. He took the fig, then smiling he said, "Did I ever tell you about the time your father and I found a beehive? No? Well, he had taken his goats out to graze one day..."

Chapter 21

The Walk

Carpus and Timothy had not gone far before they began to meet travelers headed in the opposite direction. Some were on their way to Lystra, others to points even further on the Roman highway. Carpus greeted and gave a kind word to each traveler they passed. Twice they stopped to share the latest news with people coming from Iconium. Carpus talked about the weather and asked about the happenings in Iconium. The news was the same from all accounts. Apparently, the whole town was in an uproar over some new god.

"More pagan nonsense, if you ask me," Carpus told Timothy as they continued their journey. "Power over the dead, hmph! Likely a bunch of necromancers and sorcerers spreading their lies. Don't worry, my boy, I'm sure they're nothing more than liars and thieves, trying to steal from gullible old souls that have more money than sense. That's the way of these things. Scare them with tales of the dead coming to life, then offer protection at a reasonable price. Before anyone realizes, the charlatans have moved on to the next town to find more victims and more money."

"You're probably right," Timothy said. "But isn't this yet another reason to share the truth with everyone? If they knew the true God, they wouldn't be deceived by these false prophets."

"You know," Carpus answered, "you're persistent if nothing else." Carpus laughed as Timothy gave a sheepish grin. "However, I will grant that your arguments are good, this one and the others earlier. And I understand that, from your perspective, this is important. But you've not quite persuaded me. Perhaps I'm too old to change, or maybe I'm just too stubborn. But I will say this, my son, if God speaks to you, obey His voice. Ignore this old man and follow God, but only follow God. Maybe He will choose to break His silence and send a new prophet to speak to His people. Maybe yours is the voice that God will use."

Timothy thought for a moment, then replied, "God used Daniel to be a light even when he was old."

"So, you think there's hope for me yet?" Carpus chuckled. "I'm not too old or too stubborn?"

"Well, Uncle," Timothy responded with a grin, "you're not too old."

"Ha-ha," Carpus muttered. "So old man Daniel served the Lord. I'm not sure I recall that story. Are you talking about one of his visions? Because I'm certain I don't recall all of those."

"No," Timothy answered, "I'm referring to the story of when Daniel refused to pray to the Persian king."

"Ah yes," Carpus remembered, "the time old Daniel spent a night with the lions. I like that story."

"I do too," Timothy said. "I like Daniel. He's one of my favorites from the histories of our people."

"Well, go ahead and tell the story," Carpus prompted.

"You already know the story," Timothy said. "What can I tell you that you don't know?"

"Oh, just tell the story," Carpus replied. "It'll pass the time until we get to Iconium. And maybe you'll convince me that God wants to save the pagans. I doubt it, but you can try." Carpus smiled as he gave the challenge. While he did not share the young man's high opinion of the pagans, he did enjoy the zeal with which young Timothy spoke of God. It gave him hope that God still moved among his people.

"Daniel had passed from one king to the next," Timothy began, "then from one empire to another. The Babylonians had taken him from his homeland, but now, many years later, it was the Persians who ruled the land. Daniel continued to serve both God and king faithfully and rose to the highest position. The emperor made him the highest of all the presidents and princes. Only the king himself held rank above Daniel.

"As is the case with people who seek power, those below Daniel sought to take his position from him. They looked for any fault so that they could accuse him before the king, but could find none. Daniel had dealt honestly and justly in all his business. Only in his obedience to the God of heaven could they find occasion to accuse him. You see, Daniel prayed three times a day toward Jerusalem. The other presidents and princes schemed and brought their plot before the king. They praised the king and proposed a law that all people should pray to only the king for one month's time. Anyone who disobeyed this law would be fed to the lions. The king filled with pride at the sound of their praise and foolishly signed their law.

"When Daniel heard of the new law, he didn't change his practice at all. He continued to pray to God just as he had before. But those who conspired against him petitioned the king. They accused Daniel of breaking the new law. When the king realized that his wise men had tricked him, he tried all day to free Daniel, but not even the king himself could change the laws of the Persians. They threw Daniel to the lions, but before they did, the king approached Daniel. The king told Daniel that God would save him. All that night the king could not sleep as he thought of Daniel in the lions' den. He rushed the next morning to see if Daniel had somehow survived.

"When the king called into the den, asking if Daniel's God had spared him, Daniel answered the king. He said that the angel of God had shut the mouths of the lions. Daniel was pulled from the lions' den, well and without harm. The king decreed that all those who had accused Daniel should be cast to the lions instead. They did not fare as well as Daniel. Then the king declared to his entire empire that Daniel's God was the true and living God whose kingdom will not be destroyed and whose reign will be eternal."

"Did the king really say that? I think I had forgotten that part," Carpus said. "But your story just goes to prove my point, pagans will kill us because we serve the true God. They tried to kill Daniel because he prayed to God. They only seek power and will stop at nothing to gain it. True justice was given when those who opposed Daniel were cast to the lions."

"Oh, Uncle," Timothy exclaimed, "that's not the point at all. Don't you see the effect of Daniel's faithfulness on those around him? The king of Persia was sure of God's power before Daniel was even cast into the lions' den. He was the one that told Daniel that God would save him. Where did the king learn of Daniel's God if not from Daniel's own mouth? Where others sought power and position, Daniel simply served. God placed him before the king so that he might be a witness. God revealed Himself to the king of Persia by the faithful witness of Daniel. And when Daniel faced the risk of losing that power and position which God had given to him, he didn't waver in his obedience to God. It was in his sacrifice, just like Shadrach, Meshach, and Abednego that God showed the extent of His power to save.

"When God has the power over life and death, there is nothing that His children ought to fear. We should not fear the loss of power or position. We should not fear the loss of health or wealth. We should not fear the rejection of others or the evil which they may do to us. We should not even fear the loss of our own lives. God can bless and He can heal. What people steal or destroy, God can restore and make new.

"Daniel didn't hesitate, even in his old age, to obey God. He could have decided that he wanted to die a quiet death of old age, but he could not deny his faith and his God for such a thing. And now his life serves to illuminate the path that we must walk even now as we live among the pagans. Live a faithful life in obedience to God with the hope and prayer that God will reveal Himself to the nations as He once revealed Himself to our father Abraham so long ago. We should not pray for God to destroy the pagans. We should pray that He saves them. We should not cling so dearly to this life and the things of it. Death will separate us from them whether we die at the end of a Roman sword or quietly in our bed at the end of a good, long life."

"Look!" Carpus pointed. "Iconium." The city rose in front of them. Both Timothy and Carpus quickened their pace as the city grew closer and larger before them. Carpus now dominated the conversation. The story of Daniel would have to wait. Carpus talked about his family and how happy they would be to see them. Carpus had three grandchildren. Timothy knew Carpus' grandson, Malachi. He was a bit younger than Timothy, but he was the only other Jewish boy Timothy really knew. Honestly, he did not know him well, though. Timothy had not spent much time with Malachi beyond what his mother had forced him. As children, Malachi had preferred staying at home, while Timothy had played with the other Greek boys. Both of Malachi's sisters were younger and Timothy had actively avoided them as best he could.

They soon passed the city gates and Carpus led the way toward his son's house in the market district. As they walked through the city, Timothy's eyes were wide. The city had changed since he had last been here. There were new houses and more people than he remembered. Soon they arrived at their destination. Carpus entered the courtyard and called, "Nathan! Malachi! *Sabba* is here!" Two little girls squealed and came running for Carpus. He picked them up and hugged them both. "I've missed you two so much," he said. "My, how you've grown. Now where is your father?"

"Father and Malachi are gone," Rachel replied. She was the oldest of the two girls. Leah wiggled in Carpus' arms until he put her down. She ran into the house and returned quickly with her mother.

"Miriam," Carpus exclaimed, "you look as lovely as ever. My son was lucky to find a wife like you."

"Stop it," Miriam said without emotion. "Nathan and Malachi should be home soon. They're at the synagogue listening to what that Pharisee has to say. Go on, bring your cart in. You'll want to wash I'm sure." Then she spotted Timothy behind Carpus. Her face brightened. "Timothy, what are you doing here? Is your mother here? Is she well? And Lois? How is your grandmother?"

"They're fine," Carpus answered for Timothy. "He's here to help me. I needed a good worker after my family left me all alone. Come, Timothy, let's get the cart inside."

Timothy opened the gate while Carpus led Claudius inside and back to the stable. Carpus stopped next to his son's wagon. Timothy eyed the wagon with a bit of envy. It was twice the size of Carpus' and had room for several people to ride. "Help me get his harness off," Carpus said, "then you can unload the cart. Leave the empty sacks and chests in the cart. Just take our packs and the spices out. Oh, and the figs. Take those inside to Miriam or just give them to the girls." He winked to his granddaughters, and they set out for the cart. Timothy helped remove the harness from Claudius, and Carpus led the donkey into the stall next to Nathan's two horses. Timothy began unloading the cart, working past the little girls who were already perched atop the chests, each with a fig in hand.

Just then the gate opened, and a large group of men flooded into the courtyard led by Nathan and Malachi. "*Abba*!" Nathan exclaimed. The two men embraced, then Nathan said, "It looks like you just arrived. I hope you've not been waiting long."

"No, we've just had time to bring the cart in and begin unloading," Carpus answered. "But this–what's all this?" he asked motioning to the men gathered in the courtyard.

"It's good that you've come," Nathan replied. "The whole city has gone crazy about these blasphemers."

"We heard news on the road coming in about some new god, necromancers or sorcerers. But what does this have to do with you?" Carpus questioned.

"It's not a new god, *Abba*," Nathan responded. "It's our God. These men are Jews, one of them is a Pharisee. They are proclaiming that God has a Son and that He died and was brought back to life. It's pagan blasphemy and they must be killed!"

Chapter 22

Division

Everyone spoke at once. Timothy looked around the courtyard. He took a chest from the cart and stood on it. From his vantage point he could count about twenty men standing around Carpus and his son. Some were Jews while others were Greeks. They were all speaking at once, several were shouting in deep debate. Timothy could hardly follow what any of them were saying. Carpus seemed to be having the same trouble as he shouted to the crowd to quiet. Slowly, the noise turned to a hush. Then Carpus spoke, "Now, one at a time, help me to understand. Nathan, tell me what in heaven is going on."

"About a month ago, just after you left us here," Nathan began, "two men from Jerusalem arrived as well. One of them is a Pharisee."

"Was a Pharisee," shouted one of the men behind Nathan. "He's no Pharisee anymore."

"Was a Pharisee," continued Nathan. "He stood up in the synagogue on the Sabbath to read the Scripture. Then he began to proclaim the vilest heresies."

"What if they are not heresies?" asked another man next to Carpus.

"Enough!" Nathan stopped the others. "Let me finish telling my father what has happened, then we can debate the merits of their teachings." A murmur of agreement passed through the crowd. "These men have been teaching that God had a Son and that He came to this earth. They claim that this 'Son of God' is God Himself. They say that He preached salvation to all people. They say He performed miracles as well. But they say that the Romans crucified Him. God cannot die, so this man could not have been God."

"But then they said He rose from the dead!" shouted another. "He rose from the dead so His words must be true." Again, the men broke into heated debate. Nathan threw his hands up in despair.

"Men! Men!" Nathan called. "My father has just come from Lystra and I wish to spend the evening with him. We must not decide anything tonight. I will take him to hear these men tomorrow, and then we will decide our action." The men began to leave, still debating among themselves. Some who knew Carpus came to greet him before leaving.

"Micah, you must return this evening," Nathan said to the older man dressed in religious robes. "You have been a blessing to our family for many years. You can help me tell my father of all this chaos."

"Of course," Micah replied. Then he turned to Carpus as he took his arm, "It's so good to see you again, my friend. We must serve as the voice of reason to these men."

"Yes," Carpus replied, "I only pray they listen better than we did as young men."

The last of the men had left and Carpus turned to his son. "You wanted adventure in the city. Looks like you have that and then some."

"Do I ever," Nathan said. "How are you? How is *Immah*? Shall we go inside and rest?" The two men started toward the house, then Nathan called to his son, "Malachi, help with the donkey and anything else that needs to be done."

Carpus and Nathan disappeared into the house. Malachi and Timothy greeted each other, then hurriedly unloaded the rest of the items from the cart. Neither wanted to miss the conversation that was taking place inside. Malachi gave the donkey water and some hay, then he and Timothy hurried inside. They found Carpus and Nathan inside by the fire. Carpus was still telling of their journey and of things back in Lystra. Timothy was happy he had not missed anything.

"I have to admit, I'm glad you're here," Nathan said to his father. "Your timing was perfect. I know in my heart that the right thing to do is to stone these men, but I don't know if I have the will to do it. And if we do it, the Romans will surely have something to say."

"You're sure these men have blasphemed the God of our fathers?" Timothy asked.

All eyes turned toward Timothy. "I'll forgive that comment only because you have not heard them in person," Nathan answered. "But there is no doubt that what they teach is blasphemous. They even have the audacity to call the pagans to our God. You'll see tomorrow. We'll all go to the market to hear their lies."

Timothy was about to respond to Nathan, but Carpus caught his eye. He mouthed the word, *No*. Timothy knew that Carpus was right, this was not the time to debate the call of God upon the pagans. Timothy determined that he would hear what these men had to say.

Just then Miriam placed food before the men. "I'm sure it's not as good as what your dear wife makes, but it won't kill you," she said to Carpus.

"We'll see," Carpus responded in turn.

"Must the two of you argue?" Nathan scolded. "The two dearest people in my life and you act as oil and water. Can't you get along, just for one evening?"

"I'm sorry, my son," Carpus replied first. "I'm sure it's only because I'm tired from the long journey. We will manage much better after I've rested."

"Hmph," came the reply from Miriam as she turned back to her work.

They ate the rest of the meal in silence. Timothy thought the food was delicious and Carpus didn't seem to be any worse off for eating it either. Miriam rose to light candles scattered around the room. They had only finished eating when they heard Micah's voice call from the courtyard. Nathan went out to meet the guest. Micah was not alone; he had brought his cousin with him. Micah was the same age as Carpus, but of much smaller stature and girth. His back bent from all the years he had spent stooped over studying the scrolls. Micah's cousin, Seth, did not appear to be quite as old and stood a full head taller than Micah. The two men came in and joined them by the fire. Together the six men sat around the fire, while Miriam sat on the other side of the room with her daughters.

"Thank you for coming tonight, Micah," Nathan said.

"It is a pleasure to visit a home as nice as yours," Micah replied. "In these difficult days, we must stand together with our fellow brothers."

"Micah," Carpus said, "We've known each other for years. What do you say of these men that preach in your city?"

"I say that your son gave the truth of the matter when he spoke earlier in the courtyard," Micah replied. "This Jesus of whom they speak is no more Son of God than your donkey. God has no Son and to claim such is blasphemy. Then to claim that He died and was resurrected is just scandalous. Of course, the pagans have all run after them. These Jews care not for their own blood but tell lies to anyone who will listen. It's exactly this that has the city in such chaos. They would tear down all the gods, Greek and Hebrew alike, so that all people might worship their Jesus."

"They must be stopped," Nathan added. "We heard from Antioch that they were driven from the synagogue and from the city. Now they have come here to plague us."

"And what do the other leaders of the synagogue say?" Carpus asked.

"They're divided," Micah answered. "One of them has embraced this blasphemy. Others have voiced opposition but are unwilling to stone the offenders. They are fearful of the Greeks that have followed them. They only want to expel these men from the city as those in Antioch did. The rest are with us. But we must act soon before these men turn the whole city against us."

"Father, we must do this now," Nathan said. "They betray all that is good and true."

"I must hear for myself before I condemn men to death," Carpus answered. "But if what you have said is true, then I will aid you in all that must be done."

Carpus looked around the room. Timothy's face bore a look of shock. Carpus noted that he must speak to him in private. Then his eyes settled on Seth. He had sat quietly as the others had debated. Carpus asked him, "You've been quiet, my friend. What do you say of all this? Where do you stand?"

"I'm not sure where I stand, to be perfectly honest," Seth replied.

"What do you mean?" Nathan questioned. "How can there be any doubt as to the guilt of these men?"

"I am Galilean by birth," Seth answered. "My parents raised me on the shores of the Sea of Galilee. I moved here about seventeen years ago. When I was a younger man in Galilee, there was a prophet by the name of John. I was full of zeal in those days, so I followed him. Many others heard his message and followed also. He led us to the Jordan River and preached repentance. His message was simple and clear. He told us to repent of our sins for the kingdom of heaven was at hand. Those of us who repented, he baptized in the water of the river. John told us that the Messiah was coming. The prophets Isaiah and Malachi both declared that a voice would cry in the wilderness to prepare the way of the Lord. John was that voice. We all believed it.

"Then one day, a man came to John. John declared that this man was the Messiah that God had sent. He called Him the Lamb of God, who takes away the sin of the world. Multitudes followed him, but I remained with John. I remained until we could not remain any longer."

"What do you mean? What happened?" Timothy asked.

"Herod imprisoned John, then took his head," replied Seth. "We scattered after that. Some followed the one called Messiah; I came here."

"Cursed Romans," Carpus muttered. "Another reason to hate Rome. But what does John have to do with these men here?"

"The man John named as the Messiah was called Jesus. The same Jesus, I believe, that these men now proclaim."

Chapter 23

The Message

Timothy woke with a start. Light was just beginning to peek through the window. As he looked around, he remembered where he was. There was no spare room, so Timothy had slept in the corner near the fire. Then he remembered the conversation from the night before. If what Seth said was true, then perhaps this Jesus was the promised Messiah. But Nathan and Micah had quickly dismissed everything Seth had said. They had agreed that if John prophesied of this Jesus that the Romans killed, then he was a false prophet the same as these men today. Nathan had refused to hear anything else that Seth had to say, and the evening had ended. Timothy sat up and yawned.

"Good morning," Miriam said softly from behind him. Timothy jumped. "I'm sorry, I didn't mean to startle you."

"I didn't see you," Timothy said. Miriam had wood in her arms. "Let me help you with the fire." Timothy took the wood and placed it on the fire. He stirred the embers to stoke the flames.

"Did you sleep well?" Miriam asked.

"As well as one does after a long journey," he replied.

"There is fresh water in the barrel outside," Miriam pointed toward the door.

"Thank you," Timothy said as he rose and headed for the door.

The rest of the morning passed in a blur. Nathan and Carpus hurriedly discussed the business of spice shopping. Nathan had most of what Carpus needed, but some of it they would purchase in the market. Nathan had already bought a surplus of spices in anticipation of his father's visit and stored them here at the house. They would find the rest of what Carpus needed in the market from vendors with larger selections. Nathan had already sent Malachi to open the shop. Their shop was separate from their home, unlike Carpus' back in Lystra. Their shop here was among the other vendors in the booths in the middle of the market plaza. Carpus gave Timothy a large chest filled with smaller ones along with several empty sacks to carry. They would take the empty ones to the shop on foot and only take Claudius and the cart later after they had filled them and were ready to load them. With their arms filled, the three men made their way to the market.

The market in Iconium was much larger than the one in Lystra, though the layout of the plaza was similar. Nathan led the way to the large booth where their spices were displayed. It was a suitable location, not on the outer edges where the wind would blow the spices, but not so deep within the rows of tables as to prevent customers from coming. Malachi saw them coming and hurried to help with the chests.

"Set them there behind the tables," Nathan said. The boys took the chests and stashed them behind the tables. "Has anyone been by yet?" Nathan asked his son.

"Two women purchased a few spices not long ago," Malachi replied. "Which reminds me, we're getting low on ginger and silphium."

"I'll buy some if I find them for a fair price," Nathan responded. "Anything else?"

"They've already started at the synagogue," Malachi replied.

"Already?" Nathan questioned.

"I saw them walk past. There was a large group following them too. Can I go?" Malachi asked hopefully.

"No," Nathan responded. "I need you here. You've heard their lies already. If Micah comes looking for me, tell him we've gone to the synagogue." Nathan turned back to his father, "Well, you wanted to hear the blasphemers for yourself. Let's go."

"Timothy, come along. You should hear this as well," Carpus said.

The three men continued through the maze of booths until they exited on the opposite side of the market. They were standing in front of the synagogue. It was a simple rectangular structure, nothing more than four stone walls with a large open space in the center. The building had been designed as a place for people to gather. There were no sacrifices offered here, only lessons from the Scriptures. Ordinarily, only Jews would meet here with a handful of God-fearing Greeks occasionally coming as well. Today was no ordinary day. Timothy could not even see the entrance to the building so great was the number of people trying to get inside. Both Jews and Greeks were in the crowd. As the people pushed to make their way through the crowd, the call began to bring the men out into the plaza.

"Speak in the plaza, so we can all hear!"

"Yes! In the plaza!"

"We all want to hear and see!"

Before long, the whole crowd was calling for the men to come into the open plaza next to the vendor's booths. Timothy stayed close to Carpus and Nathan as they pushed through the crowd. A shout went up from near the entrance to the synagogue.

"They're coming! They're coming!"

The crowd cheered. Nathan grabbed Carpus and Timothy by the arms. "Hurry! Let's go over there." He nodded toward the plaza. While there was no proper forum in Iconium, there was a small stone platform on the other side of the market. "That's where they'll speak." Nathan pulled Carpus toward the open area as the crowd was still surging in the opposite direction toward the synagogue. They managed to get past the crowd just as those on the edges realized what was happening and headed in the same direction as Nathan, Carpus, and Timothy. The three men managed to secure places right in front of the stage.

Within moments the crowd gathered around them. Timothy stood on his tiptoes trying to catch a glimpse of the two men as they came through the crowd. Soon enough, the crowd parted and the two men from inside the synagogue were standing on the stone platform before them. Timothy noted that neither man appeared all that different from those around him. They were ordinary men dressed in simple clothes, not in the rich robes of the other religious leaders he saw standing around.

"They don't look so dangerous," scoffed Carpus.

"Wait until they speak," Nathan replied. "Their words are more dangerous than any weapon." Nathan turned to the platform and hissed at the two men. "Blasphemers! We ought to kill you where you stand. Look at the mockery you've made of God."

Either the two men did not hear Nathan above the din of the crowd, or they chose to ignore the comments. They motioned the crowd to quiet and the noise calmed. The taller man stood before the crowd and began to speak. "Brothers, sisters, friends, we have stood among you for this last month. We have proclaimed to you the name of Jesus Christ, God's Son, and our Savior. We have explained from the Scriptures of God that He is the one sent by God to destroy sin and death. Let your ears hear and your hearts believe. Abraham looked for Him.

Moses looked for Him. David looked for Him. The prophets all looked for Him. We looked for Him. He is the one that everyone looks for. And now He is come!

"We are His messengers, sent to tell you the good news of Jesus Christ. Jesus came to preach good news to the poor. He came to heal the broken-hearted. He proclaimed deliverance to the captives. He gave sight to the blind, and he set free the oppressed. We have shown you the same signs to prove the power of God that dwells within us. We have told you all of this, but today, you must believe. You must believe in Jesus, the one that gives life everlasting.

"John proclaimed this same Jesus to be the chosen one of God, but the leaders rejected Him. Though they found no fault in Him, they killed Him. But God has raised Him from the dead. Then Jesus ascended into heaven where He stands today."

"I've heard enough," Carpus said to Nathan and Timothy, disgust written across his face. Carpus and Nathan turned to leave, but Timothy remained to hear the rest of what the man would say. "Timothy, let's go. Now!" Carpus' hand on his shoulder was firm. Reluctantly, Timothy followed them.

"There are those today who choose to reject the truth of God," the man on the platform called as they made their way out of the crowd. "Many Jews have rejected this call from God, so we have turned to all peoples to declare the work of God. Salvation will be declared to the ends of the earth."

Timothy's heart was torn as he followed Carpus through the crowd. Who was this Jesus? Something about what they had said spoke to his heart. He knew these men were not what Nathan and Micah had made them seem. Could Jesus be the answer to his prayer? Is this how God would reveal himself to Lystra? Timothy snapped back to reality as they exited the back of the crowd. Nathan and Carpus headed straight to the synagogue.

"Now do you believe all that we said last night?" Nathan asked.

"I could not believe it to be true," Carpus replied. "We must speak to those at the synagogue who remain faithful to God."

When they arrived at the synagogue there were several men gathered in the center. Micah was in the middle of them. Timothy didn't see Seth anywhere. "Carpus! Nathan!" Micah called when he saw them at the entrance. "Did you hear their lies for yourself? I pray that you are convinced now."

"I did not imagine that I would ever hear blasphemy such as that," Carpus replied. "The way they speak to the Greeks the same as the Jews, they are nothing more than charlatans."

"They are blasphemers that must be stoned!" Micah insisted.

"You must not speak of murder here in the synagogue," said one of the men behind Micah.

"Have these men not blasphemed our God? If they have, then it is not murder, but the will of God that we stone them," Micah replied.

"Still, he has a point," Nathan answered. "This is too public a place. My home is open to us. We must speak of this more. And we must gain the help of the city guard. If we do not, then we will be killed ourselves."

"I know the commander of the guard," Micah said. "It's time that we put an end to this farce."

"Agreed," Nathan said. "All who are committed to the will of God should come to my house this evening after the sun has set. Then we will make our plans."

*

Later that day, Timothy led Claudius back to Nathan's house. He had finished loading the cart with all the spices that Carpus needed. All day his mind had raced. Even now he was not thinking about the spices he had packed or the work that still needed doing. The only thought that had entered his mind all day was that he must speak to those two men. Everything else seemed so unimportant. He had to know more about Jesus. He needed to know the truth. But they were going to be killed.

The sun was sinking below the horizon as he brought Claudius back through the gate. He unharnessed the donkey, then led him into the stable. Timothy finished loading the chests into the cart as men began to filter into the courtyard. Some came alone, others in pairs. None came more than three at a time. Timothy pointed them all into the house where Nathan and Carpus were waiting. Timothy noted when Micah came that he had a Roman soldier with him. When he had loaded all the spices into the cart, Timothy went inside as well. The room was full, so Timothy remained by the door.

"I want to be rid of these men the same as you, but must you kill them? And must you do it so publicly?" the Roman asked. "Couldn't you just poison them and let them die quietly?"

"No!" Micah replied emphatically. "These men have defied the name of our God and we must stone them."

"I don't know," the Roman replied. "If you do it in the synagogue or at the market, it's likely to incite a riot."

"Are you the commander of the guard or not?" a man asked.

"I am the commander and I have no desire to put the lives of my men in danger so you can kill a couple of innocent men," the Roman replied quickly. "I should arrest the whole lot of you right now."

"These men are not innocent," Nathan said. "These men have brought the curse of God upon our whole city. The only way for us to rid ourselves of their curse is to publicly stone them."

"Curses? I want no part of any curses," the commander stated.

"Are we not reasonable men?" Micah said calmly. "I'm sure we can come to an agreement. We will take the men before first light. We'll take them out of the city, and then we'll do what we must do. It will look as if they have fled the city and no one will be the wiser."

"Then what do you ask of me?" the Roman asked.

"Just turn your eyes and the eyes of your men from what we do," Carpus said as he approached the Roman. He pressed a coin purse into the Roman's hand. "I'm sure there's enough here to close as many eyes as are needed."

Timothy could bear no more. Even Carpus was now part of this. A battle raged inside Timothy's mind. He should go to the men, warn them. Carpus would be furious. Timothy couldn't betray him after all that Carpus had done to help him. Then he remembered the words that Carpus had said on the road, "Ignore this old man and follow God." At that moment Timothy knew what he must do. He took one last look, then slipped outside into the darkness.

Chapter 24

At Night

Timothy knocked quietly on the door. The few moments he waited seemed like an eternity. When the door did open, the man who spoke in the market that morning stood before him.

"Yes?" the man said. "Can I help you, friend?"

Timothy looked over his shoulder nervously. "Don't just stand there, bring him inside," a voice called from inside the room.

"Of course," the man responded as he opened the door and allowed Timothy to pass, "come inside. We don't have much, but you're welcome to it."

Timothy stepped inside as the door closed behind him. It was just a small room with a table and two cots. The other man was sitting at the table with parchments spread across it. He set them aside and looked up at Timothy. "I'm Paul and this is my friend, Barnabas. And you are?"

"Timothy, my name is Timothy."

"Timothy," Paul asked, "how can we help you this evening?"

Timothy looked at both men, then drew a deep breath of courage. "You must leave. It's not safe for you to stay in Iconium any longer. The leaders of the synagogue have plotted to kill you. Tonight, they bribed the commander of the city guard to stay his hand when they attack you tomorrow. You must leave the city tonight!" The words spilled out so fast, he wasn't sure that the men understood the danger they faced.

Then Barnabas spoke to Paul, "I told you the scene in the market was going to be too much."

"Yes, you did," Paul replied as he gently nodded his head in agreement. "But if God wills that our lives end here, then we are ready."

"No," Timothy said. "You can't die, not yet."

"And why is that, my young friend?" Paul asked, curiously pleased at the young man's interest in his life.

"Because I must know more about Jesus," Timothy replied. "Come with me to my hometown, Lystra. It's only a day's journey from here." Paul looked to Barnabas. Timothy could not read the expressions on their faces, but it was as if the two men knew the other's thoughts.

After a moment, Barnabas shrugged and clapped his hands twice. "Let's go to Lystra," he said.

"And along the way we will tell you all about Jesus," Paul reassured Timothy.

The two men quickly packed their few belongings. Paul had a special case in which he carefully placed the parchments. Timothy watched as Paul rolled the parchments then meticulously placed them each in the case. Timothy had not seen a collection of Scriptures this size in his entire life. He thought of how his grandmother and mother would be thrilled to see such a collection of God's Word.

"Is it true that you're a Pharisee?" Timothy blurted.

Paul looked up from his task. "From an early age I was taught these Scriptures and I believed the life of a Pharisee was the only one that would please God. However, I am no longer on that path. I now follow the way of Christ. But I will answer all your questions on the road. If the danger is as you say, we must hurry before the city gates are closed."

"We should use the eastern gate, by the market," Barnabas said. "It remains open later than the others to allow for the farmers to return to their fields."

"I agree," Paul replied as he packed the last of his parchments. "That's it, I'm ready. Let's go."

They hurried through the streets of the city and exited the eastern gate just as the guards were preparing to close them. Timothy led them around to the south side of the city, and they continued off into the darkness toward Lystra. No moon shone that night to light their way, only the stars. They stayed off the road until the city lay dark behind them. As they made their way through the shadows, Timothy continued to look back, worried that Carpus would miss him and sound the alarm. Fortunately, his concerns proved to be false and eventually the three men turned toward the main road.

"I didn't think you would believe me when I came," Timothy said.

"Yours was not the first voice of warning we have heard," Barnabas said. "But it certainly was the most urgent."

"And most specific," Paul added. "Tell us, how did you come to know of this plot against us?"

Timothy's head dropped in shame. He thought of Carpus and how he had betrayed him. What would happen when they all arrived back in Lystra? Surely, Carpus would realize that he was missing, perhaps yet tonight, maybe tomorrow morning. It would not take long for him to realize what had happened. Then he would come back home to Lystra. Timothy shuddered to think of the consequences when that happened.

"I came to Iconium yesterday with a merchant, Carpus, from Lystra," Timothy replied to Paul's question. "I work for him. I came to help pack and load the spices. His son, Nathan, is a merchant here in Iconium. They are both well-connected in the synagogue. After we heard you today in the market plaza, they went to the synagogue. The leaders were plotting to stone you, but then they decided to meet tonight at Nathan's house. One of the leaders from the synagogue brought the commander of the city guard. I was by the door and heard all they planned to do. When I saw Carpus give a coin purse to the Roman, it was as if God spoke to me and I knew I had to come warn you."

"You've risked your life for us," Paul said, "and for that we are grateful. You're Hebrew? You dress and speak like a Greek."

"My mother is a Jew," Timothy replied. "My father was Greek."

"Ah," Barnabas said. "That makes sense."

"Do you follow the God of your mother or of your father?" Paul asked.

"My mother and father followed the same God. I share the same faith," answered Timothy. "I believe in the one true God of heaven, the God of Abraham, Isaac, and Jacob. My mother and grandmother have taught me the Law and the writings. I love the histories of our people. Yet I do not practice our faith as those at the synagogue do. I do not believe that God is our God alone, but He must be the God for all people, for all nations. I recognize the same in you. It's this that makes me want to hear what you have to say. You spoke to the Greeks the same as you did to the Jews. Will you tell me more about Jesus?"

Barnabas and Paul smiled at each other, then Paul began, "Much as you came to us this evening, there once was a man that came to Jesus at night. He didn't come to warn of those that would kill Him, as you did for us, but he did come looking for answers to the same questions that you ask tonight. We know this man. His name is Nicodemus. Like myself, he was a Pharisee that has now followed Jesus."

"What questions did he ask of Jesus?" Timothy prodded.

"He wanted to know who Jesus was," Paul replied. "You see, Jesus had come to the Passover feast in Jerusalem. When He entered the temple, He was appalled by the merchants who had taken residence in the house of God. He overturned their tables and drove them out. After listening to the teachings of Jesus, Nicodemus came to Him late one evening."

"He was afraid to be seen with Him, wasn't he?" Timothy asked.

"You're perceptive," Paul responded. "Yes, Nicodemus did not want people to see him with Jesus, but not because he feared for his life. He held a place among the Sanhedrin, the religious leaders. He did not want to lend authority to one that he did not understand. But he did want to understand. So, he came to Jesus to speak with Him.

"Jesus told Nicodemus that unless a person is born again, he cannot see the kingdom of God," Paul continued.

"Born again? That's impossible," Timothy objected. "What do you mean by that?"

"That's the very response that Nicodemus had," Paul laughed. "I like you, Timothy. You're a thinker. Nicodemus knew, like you, that a person is born just one time. So, he questioned Jesus again. He asked if Jesus was suggesting that a person should enter a second time into his mother's womb to be born again. Jesus replied that the second birth to which He referred was a spiritual birth. He spoke of a new spiritual beginning."

"Like when you move from knowing about God to trusting God," Timothy replied. "I think I know what you're talking about. I used to listen to the stories of God, but they never meant anything to my life. Just a few weeks ago, I chose to follow God not just because I have Jewish blood, but because I want to follow Him. I trust Him with my life. I follow God, not out of obedience, but out of faith. My obedience shows my faith."

"I do believe God sent you to us," Barnabas said. "This that you have just said is the way that Jesus showed us. To follow God in faith."

"But you must hear what Jesus said next," Paul added. "You see, Jesus was not just a teacher, or a prophet sent by God. Do you know the story of the brass serpent?"

"The one that Moses formed in the wilderness so that the people might look to it and be healed? That one?" Timothy said with a grin.

"That one," Paul replied. "Jesus told Nicodemus that even as Moses lifted up the serpent in the wilderness, so He would be lifted up. Just like God healed the people when they looked to the serpent, everyone that places their faith in Jesus will not perish, but they will have eternal life. God loves the entire world so much that He sent Jesus, the only born Son of God, so that whoever believes in Him will not perish, but have eternal life. Jesus is the one that God sent to deliver us from our sin. The spiritual birth that Jesus said that we must have comes only as one believes in Him. Just as our first birth places each of us in our respective families, this second birth places us in the family of God. Those that would be members in the family of God, must be born again by faith in Jesus."

As they walked through the night, Timothy thought about all that he had just heard. The Son of God. Jesus. Spiritual birth. Family of God. His mind raced with more questions than answers. "Is Jesus truly the Messiah? The one God promised to deliver us from sin?" Timothy asked Paul.

"Yes," Paul answered, "and He is so much more."

Chapter 25

Broken

The three men had now passed well beyond the city of Iconium and were walking the Roman highway toward Lystra. Timothy was thankful for the wide paved road on this dark night. The journey would have been more difficult if they had to travel over the rocky terrain in the dark. Timothy's mind drifted to Carpus back in Iconium. Had he noticed his absence? Would Carpus ever forgive Timothy for leaving?

"Tell me more about Jesus," Timothy said, eager for more information as well as for a distraction from his present thoughts. "Did he live in Jerusalem? Was he a rabbi at the temple?"

"Jesus was from Galilee," Barnabas answered. "He spent much of His time around the Sea of Galilee, but He also came to Jerusalem many times. I'm sorry to say that the leaders of the temple didn't like Him very much, though. They conspired against Him, much as the leaders of the synagogue did against us this night. But wherever Jesus went, He taught people about God. He did teach in the Temple and also in the synagogues, but he taught in other places as well. He spoke to the multitudes on the hillsides. He taught in houses. He stood in boats on the shores of the sea and spoke to thousands gathered around. Everywhere He went people followed Him, even more than were in the market yesterday. Jesus healed the sick and cast out demons, but His words were even more powerful than the miracles He performed."

"What could He say that was so powerful?" Timothy asked.

"It's better if I simply tell you how it happened," Barnabas answered. "Jesus was teaching in a house one day in Galilee. People had come from near and far to hear His words. Jesus had already healed several people when four men brought a lame man to Him. There were so many people in the house that day that the friends carrying the man's bed could not make their way into the house to Jesus. The only way they found to get to Jesus was to go on the roof of the house and remove the tiles. So that's what they did. They carried their friend to the roof and lowered him on his bed through the roof directly in front of Jesus.

"That must have been some sight," Timothy said. "Can you imagine doing that? They must have been certain that Jesus would heal their friend to go to such an effort."

"It was quite a sight," Barnabas said. "One that I'll never forget."

"Wait, you were there? You saw this happen?" Timothy asked.

"It was the first time I ever saw Jesus," Barnabas replied. "News had come to Jerusalem of a new rabbi that was teaching incredible things, so I went with some friends to Galilee to find Him. We were in the house when they lowered the man inside. Jesus looked at each of them and saw the man's faith and the faith of his friends. He told the man that his sins were forgiven," Barnabas continued.

"He forgave his sins?" Timothy asked immediately. "How could He do that? Only God can forgive sin."

"Exactly. We were all thinking the same thing, but Jesus knew our hearts and gave the answer before we could even give words to the thoughts," Barnabas replied. "Jesus asked which was easier, to forgive sins or to heal the lame. Then, to show that He had the authority to forgive sin, Jesus told the lame man to pick up his bed and walk."

"And did he?" Timothy asked.

"Without hesitation," Barnabas answered. "He stood and took his bed and carried it home. His friends started jumping on the roof, they were so excited. I thought the whole thing was going to come down. I was amazed at the way Jesus healed the man, but it was His forgiveness that changed me. The forgiveness of sin is a great thing, but only the person that has been wronged has the right to forgive. If I sin against my brother, then forgiveness is my brother's to give. You could not forgive me of my sin against my brother any more than I could forgive you your sin against your brother."

"But Jesus did that," Timothy replied. "He forgave the man's sin, a sin that had been committed against others."

"Yes," Barnabas replied. "So, I determined in my heart, then and there, that Jesus was either God or a lunatic. Only God or a mad man would claim to have such power, the power to forgive sins."

"But He wasn't crazy," Timothy said, "was He? He healed the lame man to prove His power."

"No, He wasn't crazy," Barnabas replied with a smile. "Jesus is God and, on that day, He demonstrated His power for all to see. When He healed the lame man, He demonstrated the power of God as His own, both to heal and to forgive. Only God has the right to forgive sin committed against others because every sin is not only against others, but also against God. Sin is a rejection of God's way. It's a failure to trust God."

"So, Jesus forgave sins," Timothy said. "The Scriptures say that the Messiah will deliver us from sin." The three men continued in silence for a while as Timothy thought about Jesus and the forgiveness of sins. Then he said, "You know, I don't have a brother. It's just me and my mother and grandmother at home."

"Jesus said that all those who do the will of God are His brothers," Barnabas answered. "When we enter into the family of God, we are all brothers and sisters."

"But you don't need to have brothers or sisters to understand forgiveness," Paul added. "Each one of us has been wronged at some point in our lives. Likewise, each one of us has wronged others. Forgiveness is that sweet reconciliation that restores relationships. It corrects what was wrong. It's like fixing something that's broken. Just as the roof was broken by the lame man's friends, so we are broken by sin. What Jesus offers is reconciliation with God. He restores our relationship with God that was ruined by the first sin in the Garden of Eden. Adam's sin brought death and destruction, but Jesus came to bring forgiveness and life. It's because of His righteousness that God will forgive us and free us from the power of sin. Sin no longer reigns over the child of faith."

"You have to tell all these things to my mother and grandmother too," Timothy said. "My mother sings all the songs that speak of the Messiah. My grandmother prays for the Messiah to come every day. You will tell them, won't you?"

"So, you believe that Jesus is the Messiah?" Barnabas asked.

"I don't understand it all, but I want to," Timothy replied. "You must tell me more."

"Timothy," Paul said as he stopped walking and turned to look at his young companion. "You must know that at a certain point it's no longer about understanding, it's about believing. Understanding will only take you so far." Paul reached out and placed his hand on Timothy's chest. "With the heart one believes unto righteousness, and out of the heart the mouth confesses that Jesus is Lord."

*

As the meeting concluded, Carpus looked around. Micah had just left with the Roman commander. There was a nervous energy that still filled the room. Nathan was speaking with some of the men that remained. Some would stay until it was time to act, others would gather at different houses to count the watches together. They would all meet at the synagogue at the beginning of the fourth watch. From there, they would go to the room that the two men had rented. They would take the men by force outside the city where they would meet their justice. By the demeanor of those standing around the room, one might never know the horrible nature of the act that had been planned only moments earlier. Though they had no legal justification to kill these men, they were convinced that God's will demanded nothing less than that they stone these blasphemers. It would not be as public as some might like, but perhaps this way was better. No sense in good men being arrested because they were following the will of God.

Carpus looked for Timothy. He had seen him standing by the door earlier. Carpus knew that Timothy would not like what was happening.

"Malachi," Carpus called his grandson over.

"Yes, *Sabba*?" Malachi answered.

"Do you know where Timothy is?" asked Carpus.

"I saw him going toward the stable. Probably looking for a good place to sleep since everyone is in here," Malachi answered. "At least that's what I'd be doing."

"Ah yes," Carpus responded, "he slept in here by the fire last night, didn't he? Thank you, my son. You should go find some rest as well."

Let Timothy sleep. This would give them something to talk about on the way home. Not that it would be pleasant, but maybe it would be better to talk when it was only the two of them. He would be able to help Timothy see the justice in what they were doing. Maybe Timothy would leave all this youthful nonsense behind him. Carpus sat down by the fire, and he too closed his eyes as he searched for a few moments of rest as well.

Chapter 26

Thirst

The road was wide and well-paved, but in the darkness, Timothy didn't see the gap between the stones. He tripped. Barnabas caught Timothy's arm just as he was falling.

"That was close," Barnabas said. "Are you okay?"

"I'm fine. I didn't see the hole. I'm afraid my sandal didn't fare so well though," Timothy replied. He held up his sandal. Two of the straps had been pulled from the sole.

"Let me see it," Paul said. Timothy gave him the shoe, then Paul said, "I can fix this." He opened his pack and searched in the darkness for a bit, then pulled a smaller pack out and opened it up. Inside was a needle and a coarse thread. "I've picked up a bit of the leather trade and always carry some supplies with me in case I need them. I should have some extra strips of leather in here somewhere," Paul said as he rummaged through his pack. "I'll have it back to new in no time," he said as he knelt down and began working on the shoe. Barnabas and Timothy stood watching Paul as he worked. "Go on you two," Paul scolded. "Watching me won't make it go any faster."

Barnabas laughed and said, "Let's go sit over there and leave the master to his work." Timothy and Barnabas walked to the other side of the road and sat on the ground. Timothy stifled a yawn. His body ached for a bed, but he knew that he needed to stay awake.

"I could splash you with some water to keep you awake," Barnabas said with a smile.

"No, thank you," Timothy said. Barnabas tried to hide his own yawn, but Timothy saw it and pulled out a waterskin from his pack. "I could splash you, if you need it."

"Who knows," Barnabas laughed, "I might let you before the night is over."

Timothy took a sip from his water then offered it to Barnabas. Barnabas drank deeply from the water and Timothy was glad that he had filled the waterskins earlier in the evening before the meeting at Nathan's house.

"You know this reminds me of something Jesus taught," Barnabas said.

"He taught you how to stay awake at night?" Timothy asked.

"No," Barnabas chuckled. "He taught about water, living water."

"Living water?" asked Timothy.

"Yes, living water. Jesus taught that He was the living water," Barnabas replied. "Jesus was on His way from Jerusalem to Galilee with His disciples. They were traveling through Samaria when they stopped at a well outside a city there. Those that traveled with Jesus entered the city to find food because it was midday, but Jesus remained at the well. While He was there, a woman from the city came to draw water. Now, Jews usually have nothing to do with Samaritans, but Jesus asked her for a drink. The woman was surprised that He would even talk to her, much less ask for help."

"But Jesus wasn't like most Jews, was he?" Timothy said. He knew too well the kind of person that would not talk to someone because of their ethnicity. Even in these modern days with all the advancements of Rome, people were still tribal when it came to foreigners. There were still those in Lystra who viewed his family as outsiders, even though they had lived there for over two decades.

"No, He wasn't," replied Barnabas. "He was most different. Jesus told the woman that if she knew who He was, she would ask Him for water because He would give her living water."

Timothy sipped again from the waterskin then asked, "How could Jesus give her water? Didn't He just ask her for water?"

"Exactly the question she asked," responded Barnabas. "She didn't understand how He could give her water either. Jesus had nothing with which to draw water, but then Jesus told her that the water He offered was not like the water from the well. Anyone who drank from the well would thirst again, but those who drink from His water will never thirst again. The water that Jesus offered would spring up into life eternal."

"That sounds great," Timothy replied. "Who wouldn't want that kind of water?"

"The woman said the same thing," Barnabas answered. "But before Jesus could give her the living water, He spoke to her about the source of her thirst."

"What do you mean, 'the source of her thirst'?" Timothy asked.

"Well," Barnabas answered, "just now, you took a drink. Why did you do that?"

"I was thirsty," Timothy answered.

"And why were you thirsty?" Barnabas asked.

Timothy thought for a moment, then replied, "We've been walking for a while, and so I was thirsty. But a person could be thirsty for many reasons. I'm thirsty when it's hot outside, or when I work hard, or when I eat something salty."

"You're right," Barnabas replied. "There's more than one reason why we are thirsty. That's the source or cause of our thirst. But there's only *one* reason why we are thirsty for living water. It's because of our sin. Just as the heat or the salt makes our bodies thirsty, sin consumes our soul and dries us out like the sun on a hot day. It leaves us in need of something to restore our soul, to make us whole. Many people try to restore themselves, hiding in the shade of a synagogue or in the corner of the temple, but only living water sent from God can restore one's soul.

"Jesus told the woman about the sin in her life. She was not married to the man with whom she lived, but she had been married to five other men. It was then that she realized that Jesus must be a prophet because what He said about her was true. When she asked Him about the Messiah that would come, Jesus told her that He was the Messiah."

"Why didn't He just forgive her sin as He did with the lame man?" Timothy asked.

"Because she hadn't yet reached the point of faith," Barnabas answered. "The lame man came to Jesus with faith and Jesus forgave him. Our sin is not automatically forgiven, we must trust Jesus to receive forgiveness. We must drink from the living water that He offers. Jesus offers the living water that satisfies the soul's thirst. When he spoke to the woman, He didn't condemn her because of her sin, He offered her living water that would restore her soul. He offered forgiveness. Jesus came to redeem her from her sin. When she did trust Him, living water flooded her soul, and she left her water pot and ran into the city to tell everyone that she had found the Messiah–the Christ. She had found forgiveness. The people of the city came out, and they heard Him and believed also. They convinced Jesus to stay two more days with them because they all wanted to hear His words of living water."

"I hate to interrupt," Paul said as he stood up, "but your sandal is ready to continue the journey." Paul handed the sandal to Timothy. Timothy placed it on his foot and secured the straps.

He gave a couple of test steps and a hop and declared the sandal good. Timothy thanked Paul and the three men continued down the road.

As they walked, Paul added, "The leaders of the temple didn't realize it, but Jesus didn't come to destroy the Jewish faith, He came to fulfill it. They were afraid of losing their power because they understood that Jesus was offering something that the law could not. The law shows us our sin. It makes us guilty before God. Jesus shows us the answer. He is the cure for the problem of sin. Just as God gave Moses water from the rock when Israel wandered in the wilderness, Jesus now offers us living water as we wander in this wilderness. We must turn to God because He is the fountain of living water."

"I think I'm beginning to understand," Timothy replied. "Jesus wants to forgive our sins, but we have to believe in Him to receive that forgiveness. It's like when you're thirsty. It's not enough that there is water in the well, you have to drink the water if you want to satisfy your thirst. But here's what I don't understand, I thought the Messiah would be a king sent to free us from Rome."

"Why do we need to be free from Rome?" Paul asked. "Just as all the other kingdoms of this earth have passed from existence, so will Rome."

"I have a friend who just told me the same thing," Timothy said. "He said that Rome, Persia, Greece, they will all be nothing but dust."

"Sounds like a smart man," Paul said.

"He's also the man who just paid the Romans, so he could kill you," Timothy replied.

"Nobody's perfect," Barnabas answered.

*

"Ahhhh!"

"Rhea!" Vitas woke with a start. He reached for his wife, but she wasn't in the bed next to him. "Where are you?"

"I'm over here," answered Rhea as she stepped into the room. "Ahhh!" She grabbed the door frame and doubled over in pain.

Vitas was on his feet in a flash. He reached out to help Rhea, "Take my arm."

"Don't touch me!"

Vitas pulled back his arm. "What can I do? Should I get Eunice?"

Rhea stood holding the doorpost for a moment. Vitas stood in the darkness unsure of what he should do. "Now, give me your arm," Rhea said suddenly. Vitas quickly helped Rhea back to the bed.

"Where did you go?" Vitas asked.

"I was thirsty. I went to get a drink, but I didn't make it," she answered. Vitas quickly went to the courtyard and filled a cup with water. Rhea drank it and asked for another. After the second cup, she said, "You can get Eunice now." Vitas looked at her, worried if he should leave her alone. "I'm fine. Go!"

Chapter 27

Hunger

When Timothy had passed this way with Carpus, the hot sun had beat down upon them. Now as he returned to Lystra, only the cold stars shone in the sky above. Timothy felt a chill as a cold gust of air passed over him. He shivered and wished that he had a heavier coat. Even now, just before harvest, the nights were cold. Cold and tired, Timothy's mind still raced with thoughts of Jesus. Messiah. Living water. Forgiveness of sin. Born again. What did all this mean?

"So, if Jesus was the Messiah, why didn't the temple leaders and everyone else follow Him?" Timothy asked.

"Because to follow Christ is to deny one's own self. Few are willing to do that," Paul replied. "They would have had to submit their authority to Him. Besides, they had their expectations of what the Messiah should be and should do. Many looked for a conquering king to defeat Rome, as you mentioned earlier. But it is not from Rome that we need freedom. We are captives to sin and to death. Jesus came to deliver us from sin. He came to give us life. To put your faith in Jesus means that you have to let go of your own ideas and follow Christ regardless of the cost we must pay."

"Jesus answered this question Himself after He fed the multitude," Barnabas added.

"Jesus fed the multitude? What do you mean?" Timothy asked.

"He was in Galilee with His disciples when the multitude followed Him once again. He had healed many among them, and they came to Him to see what else He would do," Barnabas continued. "They had no food to give the people, except for a small lunch of bread and fish. The Lord commanded the people to sit down. Once they sat down, Jesus broke the fish and bread and gave it to all so that they might eat."

"How many people were there?" Timothy asked.

"They counted 5,000 men," Barnabas replied.

"Five thousand! And Jesus fed them with only a single lunch?" Timothy questioned.

"Five loaves and two small fish is all they had. When they had all eaten their fill, the disciples collected twelve baskets full of food," Barnabas answered.

"But, that's a miracle!" Timothy gasped.

"Yes, it was," said Barnabas. "Only one of the many that Jesus performed. But the answer to your question, why people didn't follow Him, came the next day. In the night, Jesus had crossed to the other side of the sea. That's a whole other story," Barnabas said as he glanced at Paul, "maybe we can tell you later. Anyway, the people chased after Jesus and found Him that next day. Jesus confronted them. He accused them of chasing after Him because He filled their bellies with food, not because they wanted to see miracles. He told them not to work for food that perishes, but to work for the food which endures to life eternal."

"What did He mean by that?" Timothy asked.

"He said that we should believe in Him, the One that God sent," Paul responded.

"Jesus said that He was the bread of life," Barnabas continued.

“Hold on, let me get this straight,” Timothy stopped walking. Paul and Barnabas stopped also and turned to Timothy. “Bread of life, living water, feeding thousands with a single lunch? My friend Vitas is going to love you guys.”

“Can’t wait to meet him,” Barnabas chuckled. “I’m guessing he likes food?”

“I’ve been teaching him about the Passover meal, and he’s been talking about doing a practice run, as an excuse to butcher another lamb,” Timothy said.

“Oh, I like him already,” Barnabas replied.

“Okay, so Jesus is the bread of life,” Timothy said as they continued walking. “I’m guessing this is another picture like living water. Why wouldn’t people want to believe in Jesus? He was offering eternal life and forgiveness of sins, and He explained it using easy things to understand like bread and water. Everybody needs food and water, exactly like we need forgiveness and eternal life.”

“Well, that may be,” said Barnabas, “but the people weren’t ready to believe yet. They said that their fathers had eaten manna in the wilderness, so they asked Jesus for a sign that they might believe Him also.”

“What! Didn’t He just feed them the day before?” Timothy replied. “Weren’t they paying attention? How could they forget so soon?”

“Timothy, you’re absolutely correct,” Barnabas replied. “He had just fed them. Jesus reminded them that it wasn’t Moses who gave the manna, but God in heaven who did. Exactly like the Father has now given us the true bread. Jesus, the one who gives life eternal.”

“All who believe in Jesus will never hunger or thirst again,” Paul added. “This doesn’t mean that their bodies won’t hunger or thirst. It does mean that the eternal life that Jesus gives will satisfy the hunger and thirst of their souls forever.”

"We must commit our trust to Jesus," Barnabas replied. "He said we must eat and drink His body and blood. In Him is eternal life. It doesn't always make sense. It's a messy picture that He gave, to think that the hunger and thirst of our soul is satisfied only by eating and drinking of Jesus, but that's the picture He gave us by calling Himself the living water and the bread of life. Our bodies eat and drink of the bread and water of this earth, and we still die. Those that eat and drink of Jesus Christ, their souls will live forever."

"But most people only want their bellies filled, don't they?" Timothy stated. "They live and die without ever considering their souls. But God wants to restore our souls, to lead us in the paths of righteousness. Is that the way of Jesus?"

"You are wise beyond your years, Timothy," Paul said.

"My grandmother says that wisdom comes from obeying the voice of God," Timothy replied. "I've never heard God speak like the prophets did, but I feel like this whole week He's been speaking to my heart."

The three men continued walking through the night. The cool air settled all around them. Timothy fought a yawn, but his body was tired. The adrenaline rush of fleeing the city had kept his body from feeling the lateness of the hour. The stories of Jesus had kept his mind racing, but now he needed to lay down. Only a few moments of rest, and he would be ready to continue their journey home. Barnabas and Paul sensed the same. Just then Timothy saw a familiar wooden structure rising in the night.

"Look, it's the old Roman well," he exclaimed. "We're halfway to Lystra."

*

"*Abba*," Nathan nudged Carpus as he slept in the chair. "It's time to go."

Carpus rubbed his eyes and yawned as he stretched his arms. He took the lamp his son handed him and stood to his feet. "Let's go. The sooner we do this the better."

"Should we call Timothy?" Nathan asked.

"No, his heart is not with us," Carpus responded. "It's better that he sleeps than cause problems after we've begun."

Carpus looked around. Nathan had kept watch with four others. Malachi was with them also, but looked as if he too had just awoken. Together the men made their way to the synagogue, careful not to raise their voices. When they arrived at the synagogue, Micah was already there, dressed in his Sabbath robes. Truly, this was the righteous thing to do. Soon there were twenty men gathered, mostly Jews, but also a few Greeks. They waited until the fourth watch had sounded, then made their way across town armed with torches and the righteousness of their cause.

They called into the room for the men to come out. When they didn't answer, Carpus motioned two of the men to break the door. The door burst as they rammed into it. Nathan and several others rushed into the room to capture the blasphemers. Carpus could hear the shouts as he stood outside. Chaos reigned as the men shouted inside. Carpus could not tell what was happening until Nathan stepped into the light.

"They're gone!" he said. "They've taken their things and the beds have not been slept in. Someone must have warned them."

"I must have words with that commander," Micah exclaimed. "He was the only one that knew of our mission."

"You're sure they are gone? This is the right room?" Carpus asked.

"This is the room. They have been here all month," Micah replied.

"Cowards! Maybe it's for the best that they've gone," Carpus said. "We have no blood on our hands, and they've disappeared like the charlatans we knew them to be."

"Perhaps," Micah answered. "But we should not be so sure that they won't continue their blasphemies in nearby villages. I'll speak to the commander and find out when these men left. One of his guards must have seen them."

"Very well," Carpus said. "You speak to the commander, and then we will meet back at my son's house." Then turning to Nathan and Malachi, "Come, let's go home. There's nothing more to do here." The rest of the men followed Micah and Carpus' example and returned to their homes.

"They likely fled back to Antioch," Nathan said as he warmed himself by the fireplace. "From there they'll return to the coast and catch a ship back to Jerusalem."

"We can only hope that we see no more of them," Carpus answered.

"They have proven to be cowards, nothing more than liars," Nathan said with an air of satisfaction.

"Could it be that God sent them away, so they wouldn't be killed?" asked Malachi quietly.

"It is God's will that we kill them," Nathan replied hastily, satisfaction now replaced with anger. "It was only the work of evil that they escaped from our hands this night."

"Why don't you go wake Timothy for me, my son?" Carpus said to Malachi. The boy meekly exited the room. Once he was gone, Carpus said to Nathan, "He's young. He had no desire to kill those men, regardless of the merit. You should not be so hard."

"No, *Abba*," Nathan replied, "he must not be weak when it comes to the law. You were not so slack in your conviction when I was a boy. You wouldn't have accepted that kind of rebellion in me, I will not allow it in Malachi. He must understand that justice must be done."

Silence filled the room. Only the crackling of the flames broke the stillness of the early morning. Carpus looked into the fire and watched as the flames danced across the wood. A few moments later, Malachi returned.

"*Sabba*, I can't find Timothy anywhere. I've looked in the stable and in all the rooms. He's not in the courtyard. He's not here."

"Nonsense," Nathan scolded. "He must be here somewhere. People don't disappear in their sleep."

Carpus turned and looked out into the courtyard. He thought of the events of the last day. He never did have that chance to talk to Timothy. Suddenly, understanding spread across his face. "Nathan," Carpus said, "I think I know where Timothy is."

Just then Micah burst into the courtyard. The commander followed Micah along with two guards.

"Carpus! Carpus!" Micah shouted.

Carpus and Nathan stepped outside. The soldier's torches cast a bright glow about the courtyard. Micah was bent over, hands on his knees, trying to catch his breath. Apparently, they had run all the way to Nathan's house.

"Micah, my friend," Carpus exclaimed. "What's the matter? What is it?"

"Where's your man?" Micah gasped. "The one you brought from Lystra?"

"We can't find him," Carpus said. "We thought he was sleeping in the stable, but he's nowhere to be found. I'm not sure where he is. Why?"

"I questioned my men," the commander answered. "One of the guards saw him. He left the city through the farmer's gate before it closed last night."

"He left," Carpus whispered, stunned that Timothy had returned home without him.

"You old fool!" Micah cried when he saw the confusion on Carpus' face. "He didn't leave alone. He left with the blasphemers! Your man is the one that helped them escape!"

Chapter 28

The Way

Paul and Timothy sat on the rocks near the well. Barnabas was sleeping, stretched out nearby on the ground.

"Does he always go to sleep that fast?" Timothy asked.

"Usually," Paul replied. "He says he has to sleep first, or he'll be awake listening to me snore all night."

"How long have the two of you been traveling together?" Timothy asked. "I mean how long have you known each other?"

"We left Antioch about eight months ago," Paul replied. "Not Antioch here, Antioch of Syria."

"I thought you were from Jerusalem?" Timothy said. "That's what I heard them saying earlier, at least."

"I'm originally from Tarsus, and Barnabas is from Cyprus, but it's true that we've each spent a great deal of our youth and adulthood in Jerusalem," Paul answered. "We actually first met in Jerusalem when we were much younger, before Jesus. I didn't know Barnabas well, but we were both students in the temple. After Jesus came, Barnabas followed the way, but I persecuted those who followed Jesus. The truth is that I was more zealous than those who threatened us this night. Few escaped from my hand. But God stopped me and spoke to me. He opened my eyes and brought me from darkness into the light and forgave my sins. After my conversion, Barnabas was the one that introduced me to the other believers in Jerusalem. Eventually, I returned to Tarsus while he stayed in Jerusalem. Then some years ago, many of the followers of Christ moved to Antioch. Barnabas was sent from Jerusalem to teach and guide the church. He brought me from Tarsus to help him. We've been ministering together ever since. Anyway, that's our story, the short version at least."

"That's why you're not mad or afraid of those that want to kill you," Timothy said. "Because you used to be like them."

"I used to lead them," Paul said. Timothy could hear the regret in Paul's voice. "That's certainly part of it. I'm sorry to say that many followers of the way of Christ died because of my actions. I was convinced that I was obeying the will of God. But God has forgiven me of even this sin, and He has given me eternal life."

"How does one come to receive eternal life?" Timothy asked.

"There was a rich young ruler who asked Jesus the same question," Paul answered. "This man believed himself to be righteous because he had kept the law from his youth. He wanted to know if this was enough to gain eternal life. I was much the same as him. I too had kept the law from my youth. What neither he nor I understood was that the law cannot save us, it can only show us where we come short of God's glory."

"So, what did Jesus tell him?" Timothy asked.

"Jesus told him to sell all his possessions and give them to the poor. Jesus called him to follow Him," Paul replied. "The young man left in sorrow because he was extremely wealthy. Jesus told those that were there that it is difficult for the rich to enter into the kingdom of God."

"I understand that we should give to the poor," Timothy stated. "But why did Jesus tell him to give away his wealth? If he had kept the law since his youth, surely his wealth was a blessing from God. Hadn't God blessed this man with his riches?"

"God does bless with wealth and health and many other things that cannot be measured," Paul replied. "But the sinful condition of our heart often leads us to place those blessings from God before God in our worship and our trust. A rich man trusts in his wealth the same as a young man trusts in his strength. If anyone places their trust in those things rather than in God, then they've misplaced their trust. Eternal life does not come by our wealth or by our poverty. Eternal life comes only from Jesus. That is why Jesus told the man to give away all he had and to follow Him. Only by turning from our ways and placing faith in Jesus does one gain eternal life."

"But if the rich cannot be saved," Timothy countered, "then who can?"

"I did not say that the rich cannot be saved," Paul answered, "and neither did Jesus. Jesus said it would be difficult, but nothing is impossible with God. There was another rich man, a tax collector in Jericho called Zacchaeus, who wanted to see Jesus. He tried to make his way through the crowds, but he was a man of small stature. He could not see past the crowds or push his way through them. He saw a tree farther along the path that Jesus walked. Zacchaeus hurried to the tree and climbed up into it."

"Wait, a tax collector climbed up into a tree?" Timothy questioned. "Like a child would?"

"Yes," Paul laughed, "I imagine it must have been quite a sight."

"I can see him now, pulling up his robes so he could climb the tree. I've never seen a rich man do anything like that," Timothy said. "So, did he see Jesus? After he climbed the tree?"

"More than that," Paul replied. "As Jesus came close, He stopped and spoke to Zacchaeus by name. He said that He would stay at Zacchaeus' house that day."

"Jesus went to his house?" Timothy said slightly shocked. "A rabbi or Pharisee would never go to a tax collector's house."

"You're right," Paul responded, "they wouldn't. But Jesus was no Pharisee nor was He any ordinary rabbi. Many murmured against Him because He entered and ate in the house of this sinner."

"Then why would Jesus do such a thing? I don't understand," Timothy said.

"Because Jesus didn't care about outward appearances. It didn't bother Him what the Pharisees said about Him. Jesus cared about those that needed Him. You see, when Jesus went to Zacchaeus' house, Zacchaeus followed Jesus. He repaid four times all that he had taken unlawfully from others. Salvation came that day to Zacchaeus' home. Timothy, let me ask you a question. Who needs a doctor?"

"A sick person needs a doctor," replied Timothy.

"Exactly. And who needs to be found?" Paul asked.

"Someone who's lost, I suppose," Timothy answered.

"Jesus came to heal the sick and to bring home the lost. He came to call sinners to repentance. That's why He went to the tax collector's house," Paul said. "If you want to save the lost, you must go to where they are. That's what Jesus did. He didn't join in their sins or become like them, but He called them to repent of their sins and to come to Him. And many did."

Barnabas stirred then slowly sat up. "Good morning, how long did I sleep?" he said as he yawned.

"An hour, maybe two," Paul replied. "The sun will be up soon. Are you ready to go?"

"Let me refill our waterskins," Barnabas replied as he stood to his feet. Soon he had filled the skins, and they were back on the road, headed for Lystra. "What did I miss while I was sleeping?"

"I think the Pharisees were wrong," Timothy said.

"I don't disagree with that, but do you mind explaining how you came to that conclusion? I still think I'm missing part of your conversation," Barnabas said.

"I told him about Jesus with Zacchaeus," Paul answered.

"Ah, okay," Barnabas replied. "It's beginning to make sense. So, how were the Pharisees wrong, Timothy?"

"They criticized Jesus for eating with the tax collector because he was a sinner, but we are all guilty of sin before God," Timothy answered. "That's what you said the law does, show us where we fall short. Zacchaeus was a sinner, but so were the rest of them, Pharisees included. Right?"

"Yes," Paul answered. "We're all sinners. We've inherited sin as part of our nature from Adam, but we each commit our own sin that separates us from the righteousness of God."

"Zacchaeus knew he was a sinner and went searching for Jesus," Barnabas added. Then Barnabas smiled and nodded toward Paul, "It takes Pharisees a bit longer to figure out that they're sinners. They think they're so smart, but really they're not."

"Ha ha," Paul said. "You're so funny."

"But when they do figure it out," Barnabas added, this time more serious, "God will save even one who has killed His children."

"Amen to that," Paul said.

*

"Is she okay?" Vitas stuck his head inside and asked. "I heard her scream again."

"If that man comes in here again, I'm going to scream," Lois said while casting a glare toward Vitas. Vitas had brought Eunice and Lois to help Rhea, but since their arrival he had hovered around them, more in the way than helpful.

"Vitas," Eunice said kindly as she ushered him back into the courtyard, "I know you're concerned for Rhea, but there's nothing you can do. I promise you, there is nothing unusual so far, only the normal pains of childbirth. This is not the first time we have helped to bring new life into this world. We will take care of Rhea and you will soon have a child to celebrate."

"Tell him to stay in the courtyard with Horace," Lois shouted from inside. "At least that one has the good sense to stay out there."

"You're sure she's okay?" Vitas asked. It was not quite daybreak, but he was already dripping with perspiration.

"She's fine, I promise," Eunice comforted.

"Come on, Vitas," Horace said. "Take me out to the city gates. I want to welcome the new day."

"Now?" Vitas asked. "You want to go now?"

"Yes," Horace replied firmly. "Can't you see, they don't need you here right now. We're just in the way. We can watch the sunrise and maybe hear some news from the other men out there."

"Fine," Vitas replied. "I'll take you, but I'm not staying long."

Thank you, Eunice mouthed to Horace.

Chapter 29

The Father

Sunlight broke past the horizon as the three men made their way down the highway. They had moved slowly in the dark, but would soon arrive in Lystra. Timothy was anxious to see his mother and grandmother. There was so much he had to tell them. He hoped they would understand and forgive him for leaving without Carpus. They would understand once they heard what Barnabas and Paul had to say. Timothy knew that the difficult part would be explaining to Carpus why he had done what he had. Then a different problem presented itself in Timothy's mind.

"I don't suppose either of you speak Lyconian, do you?" Timothy asked.

"Lyconian?" Barnabas responded. "Is it like Greek or Aramaic? I'm afraid those are the only languages we speak."

"It's got some Greek in it," Timothy answered. "Many people in Lystra will understand you when you speak Greek, but you may not understand everything they say. I'll translate for you, if you need it."

"We'll keep you close," Barnabas smiled as he wrapped his arm around Timothy's shoulders.

"Let me make sure I understand all that you have said in case I do need to translate something," Timothy said. "You said that we must be born again. That means that we enter the spiritual family of God. You said that Jesus can forgive our sins because He is God. It's like eating and drinking, but only Jesus can satisfy the hunger and thirst of our soul. All our wealth and strength doesn't matter if we don't seek after God. Only Jesus can give us eternal life."

"Sounds about right," Paul answered. "Jesus is God made flesh, come to cleanse us of our sin and to make us right with God. We must call on the Lord Jesus Christ, and He will save us."

"There is something I don't understand. Why would God do this?" Timothy said. "Why would Jesus bother with the tax collectors and the sinners? Why didn't He just teach the religious leaders and let them teach the rest of us?"

"Because that's who God is," Paul replied. "He comes directly to the sinner. He rejoices in the sinner who repents. Even though we have turned our backs on God, God still loves us. Jesus answered this question when He spoke to the Pharisees. He said that a shepherd with one hundred sheep would search after just one if it was lost. He would leave the ninety-nine safe at home and go out to find the one that had gone astray. Then He rejoices more over the one that He finds than the others that are safe at home. Heaven rejoices the same over a single sinner that repents and turns to God."

"Then Jesus told of a woman who had ten silver coins," Barnabas added. "She lost one, and so she diligently searched her house until she found the one that was lost. When she found the coin, she called her friends together and rejoiced with them. The angels of God rejoice the same when a sinner repents."

"Jesus told the Pharisees another story of a father with two sons," Paul continued. "The younger son came to his father and asked for his inheritance. So, the father divided his property and gave the younger son his part. The son took all his wealth and left for a distant land. There he wasted all he had on reckless living. When he had spent all his riches, a famine came upon the land. The son found work taking care of pigs. When he saw that the pigs had more to eat than he did, he remembered his father. He decided to return home, not as a son, but as a servant in his father's house. At least then he would have food to eat."

"That would have been humiliating," Timothy interjected, "to have left in pride only to return in shame. I wouldn't know what to say."

"Neither did the son, so he rehearsed what he wanted to say to his father, even before he arrived home," Paul answered. "He wanted to tell his father that he had sinned against him and against heaven. No longer was he worthy to be called a son, but he would be a hired servant."

"Wow," Timothy exclaimed. "And then what happened?"

"As the son returned home, the father saw him coming from a far distance," Paul said. "The father was moved with compassion and ran to his son. He embraced him and kissed him. The son said to his father, 'I have sinned against heaven and before you. I am no longer worthy to be called your son.' Before he could finish, the father called for his servants. He dressed him in the finest robes. He put a ring on his finger and shoes on his feet. He called for the servants to kill the fatted calf and threw a feast for his son. The father rejoiced because this son who had been dead, was alive again. The son who had been lost, now was found."

"The son didn't even have a chance to tell his father that he would work as a servant," Timothy remarked. "The father was so happy to have him back."

"That's how our Father, God, is with us," Paul replied. "He is the Good Shepherd that seeks after the lost sheep. He is the one who searches for the lost coin. He is the one who rejoices in his son's repentance. God wants His lost children to return home to Him, so He sent His Son to the earth to call all to repentance."

"But not everyone will turn to God, will they?" Timothy asked.

"No, not everyone will return to the Father," Paul answered. "The other brother in the story, the older brother, had remained faithful to the father. He stayed at home while his brother wasted his life. Yet, when his brother returned home, he would not enter into the celebration. His father came out to him. The older brother complained to his father that he had obeyed his every command, yet had never received so much as a goat for him and his friends. He was mad that his father was celebrating the return of the younger brother."

"Just like the Pharisees," Timothy said. "They were mad that Jesus was feasting with the sinners. They didn't understand that Jesus was celebrating the return of the lost son."

"Like the older brother, they had stayed close to the Father. They thought that keeping the laws of Moses would make them right, but they had never experienced the joy of the Lord," Paul said. "I know, I was like that. Following God is more than knowing and keeping the rules. Following God is sharing in His joy when the sinner repents and returns home."

"I want to follow Jesus too," Timothy said, stopping in the middle of the road. "I don't know everything and I probably never will, but I know I'm a sinner and I know that only God can save me. I'm ashamed of the sin I've committed, but if Jesus will have me, I'd like to put my faith in Him too."

"But you've not even heard the good part," Barnabas said, "the part about His death and resurrection."

"If Jesus truly was the Messiah and if He is the only way to eternal life, then He is the one I have been looking for," Timothy answered. "And if the good part is His death and resurrection, then I look forward to hearing it too, but I already believe it. You say that Jesus died and God brought Him back to life; I accept it as true. What must I do to be saved?"

Paul looked at Timothy and said, "Believe in the Lord Jesus Christ and you will be saved. Confess with your mouth the belief in your heart and God will grant you eternal life."

"I believe," Timothy said. Then he lifted his eyes to heaven, "God in heaven, hear me. I believe that Jesus is the Messiah, sent to defeat sin and death. I want to drink the living water and eat the bread of life. Forgive my sin and give me new life, eternal life." Timothy stopped and looked at Paul. "Is that it?"

Paul's smile said it all, "That's it, but that's only the beginning of your new walk, brother."

"Ahh, come here," Barnabas said. He wrapped his arms around Timothy and lifted him off the ground in an embrace. "The angels are rejoicing in heaven; we should celebrate here on earth as well!" He set Timothy down, then said, "This talk of celebrating has made me hungry. How much longer before we get to Lystra?"

"It's the city on that hill. Can you see it?" Timothy answered as he pointed to the city. The morning sun was now high enough that the city was plainly visible."

"Great, let's get moving," Barnabas said. "You think you can help us find something to eat when we get there?"

"I'm sure my mother has something that we can eat," Timothy said. He sniffed the air, "I can smell it already."

*

The news spread fast. The sun had not even risen, but everyone knew that the blasphemers had been aided by Carpus' man. Nathan had been furious. He could not believe that one in his own house had helped the blasphemers escape. Micah had called Carpus' own allegiance into question. Carpus was in shock. First, he had denied that Timothy was gone. He had searched the stables and the house again. Finally, after finding no sign of Timothy and at Micah's continued insistence, he had accepted that Timothy had indeed helped the men escape. Then his anger had grown, first at the shame of Timothy's betrayal, but then with the recognition that Timothy would take the men to Lystra. They would spread this blasphemy in his hometown. He must do something about it.

Carpus looked around. There was still an hour before the sun would rise, but the synagogue was filled with men. He recognized many of them. All those who had been part of the plot were there. There were also other men, Jews who had stood with the blasphemers. Apparently, someone had told of their failed attempt and now the synagogue was filled with the bickering of the two sides.

"You should not have made an attempt on their lives without the full support of the synagogue!" shouted one.

"God wills that the blasphemers be stoned," Micah demanded.

"God allowed them to escape from out of your hands, betrayed by one of your own," came the reply.

"Enough," shouted Carpus. The room quieted. All eyes turned to Carpus as he stood above the men. "It is true that my man led the blasphemers out of the city." Whispers filled the room. "But I believe he was misled by the zeal of youth. He has now led these men to my city, Lystra, where they will deceive many. There is no synagogue to stand against these men and counter their lies. I will leave immediately, with any who are willing and likeminded, to finish what we have started this day. Our God is one God. He has no son and He cannot die. These blasphemers *must* die."

He finished and walked out of the synagogue. Micah and Nathan were by his side. Several others fell in behind him including some who had come from Antioch. They headed in unison back toward Nathan's house.

"Micah! Carpus!"

They paused to see who was coming after them. It was Seth, Micah's cousin. He hurried to catch up to them.

"Cousin," Micah said, "do you come to join us?"

"Don't do this, Micah," Seth said. "I fear that your fight is not against men, but against the Almighty Himself. You will not prosper in your way."

"Have you believed their lies also?" Micah replied. "Be gone! You're no family of mine."

"I beg you, do not go," Seth called, but only silence replied. He turned to the others, "Carpus, Nathan, brothers, leave these men in peace."

"There will be no peace until God's judgment has been given," Carpus said then pushed past Seth. The others followed Carpus, pushing past Seth and mocking him. One of the men knocked Seth to the ground and spit on him. Seth rose to his knees in the middle of the dusty plaza and cried out to heaven, "Forgive them!"

Chapter 30

Lystra

Several men stood gathered at the city gate. Many were preparing to go out into the fields to work, but others gathered around sharing stories and telling jokes. As they climbed the hill toward the gates, Paul said, "I believe God has prepared an audience for us."

Barnabas took a look at the men gathered at the gates. "I spoke in the marketplace yesterday. It's your turn today."

"You're going to speak to the men here at the gates?" Timothy asked.

"Is there a synagogue in the city?" Paul asked.

"No," Timothy replied. "There are only two Jewish families in the city, Carpus' and mine. The only religious building is the Temple of Zeus, just inside the city gates."

"Then we will testify to the men gathered here at the gates of the city," Paul responded.

The men at the gate had turned their eyes upon the strangers walking toward them. One cried out, "Greetings, travelers!"

"Greetings!" Barnabas replied to the men at the gates.

"You traveled the road at night. From where do you come?" asked another of the men.

"We come from Iconium," Paul replied. "Our friend desired to return home to his city, so we joined him." Timothy saluted the men. He knew some of their faces, and they returned the recognition.

"What news do you bring from Iconium?" another man asked.

"We bring news not from Iconium, but from the God of heaven," Paul began. "We have come to deliver a message of hope that all people might be delivered from the darkness of sin into the light of God's love."

Barnabas leaned in and whispered to Timothy, "Be ready to translate if it seems they don't understand."

"I will be," Timothy whispered. "Let's see how it goes."

Paul had continued speaking while Timothy and Barnabas conversed, but now he stopped. His eyes were fixed on something, or someone, but Timothy could not see from where he was standing. Paul started moving toward the crowd, then as the men stepped back, Timothy saw him. Paul was looking at Horace. Horace was sitting, leaning against the gates. His eyes were fixed on Paul. Timothy had seen that look before. Paul stopped and spoke directly to Horace, "Stand upright on your feet."

Horace's eyes never broke with Paul's. Timothy watched in awe as Horace jumped to his feet in one swift, strong motion. The man who had never taken a step in his life walked toward Paul. Timothy ran to Horace and wrapped his arms around him.

"Horace!" Timothy shouted. "You're walking!"

"I'm walking!" Horace cried, tears streaming down his face. "Timothy, praise God, I'm walking."

The men crowded around Timothy and Horace. Some were shouting in amazement, others were grasping at Horace, trying to see his legs. Others surrounded Paul and Barnabas. People from the city quickly began to join the crowd, drawn by the commotion.

“Horace,” Timothy grabbed his friend and tried to push the crowd back. He shouted in his ear, “We have to go tell Vitas!”

“Rhea!” Horace shouted in reply. “She’s having her baby!” Timothy could not hear what Horace said next, but then he heard Horace shout, “I’ll race you home!” The smile on Horace’s face shone brighter than the sun as he pushed through the crowd and took off down the street like a child. Timothy looked back to where Paul and Barnabas had been. The crowd had surrounded them also and Timothy could no longer see them. He turned and chased after the cripple who was now running through the city streets.

*

“Where’s Timothy?” Paul shouted to Barnabas. He tried to free himself as the crowd pushed up against him.

“He went to the cripple,” Barnabas answered, trying to make himself heard over the uproar, “but I can’t see either of them now.”

“I can’t understand what they’re saying,” Paul yelled. “Can you?”

“Can you understand what they’re saying?” Barnabas called in reply. “I can’t make out anything.”

Paul shook his head. He couldn’t understand anything the crowd was shouting, nor could Barnabas apparently. He whispered a prayer to heaven, then he turned to the crowd and called out in Greek for the crowd to quiet. Those immediately next to Paul and Barnabas fell to the ground. Others behind them did likewise. Soon the whole crowd was on the ground, silent before them.

“Well, they’re quiet,” Barnabas shrugged.

Paul called to the crowd, “Do not worship us. We are men like you are.” He grabbed one of the men before him by the arm and tried to lift him to his feet. The man hesitantly rose. "We come to proclaim the God of heaven to you. The God who healed the cripple can make you whole." The man fell back to the ground as soon as Paul removed his hand.

"I don't think they understand what you're saying," Barnabas said.

*

"Vitas!" Horace called as he burst into the courtyard. "Vitas, where are you?"

"I'm in here," Vitas answered. The voice came from the stable. "The women won't let me inside. Hey, how did you get back home?"

Vitas stepped into the courtyard from the stable. He looked at Horace. Then he looked again. Horace was standing in the center of the courtyard.

"Wh…How?" stammered Vitas.

Tears poured down Horace's face. "Timothy," he managed to say between the tears.

"Timothy?" Vitas asked.

"Is Timothy back?" Eunice called from in the house. "Did I hear you say Timothy had returned?" she said as she stepped into the courtyard. She froze in the doorway, her eyes fixed on Horace.

Vitas rushed to Horace and swept him into a grand embrace. Eunice called Lois to come out.

"What's all the fuss out here?" Lois said as she stepped outside. She saw Horace standing next to Vitas. "Praise God almighty!" she shouted.

"What's going on?" Rhea shouted from in the house.

At that moment, Timothy burst into the courtyard from the street. "Horace can walk!" he shouted. "Horace can walk!"

*

The crowd began to shout again, but now they cried out in unison. Their chants were unknown to Paul and Barnabas. Paul repeatedly tried to quiet the crowd, but every time one part of them would quiet, the chant would begin anew from some other part. “We are Jews,” he cried out. “We come to proclaim the God who made the heaven and the earth and the sea.”

“I don’t think they are listening,” Barnabas said. The crowd suddenly quieted. Barnabas motioned to the back of the crowd, “Look, here comes someone.”

A small parade was making its way through the crowd. A round man in an elaborate purple tunic led several temple acolytes through the crowd. The acolytes were young men and women that served in the temple. Behind the acolytes several men followed, each one leading a bull.

“This must be the local priest. We must be careful,” Paul said.

The priest came and stopped directly before Barnabas. He bowed himself to the ground. The temple acolytes followed suit. Paul called them to rise to their feet. The priest looked up, confusion on his face. Paul reassured him that he was to rise. Slowly, the priest rose to his feet. Paul addressed him, “We are men sent from God. We deliver a message to you and your city. God has sent a sacrifice to deliver all humanity from the bondage of sin.”

“God, yes. Message, yes. Sacrifice, sin, yes,” the priest replied. His Greek was obviously limited. He turned to the crowd and delivered a short speech in Lyconian. Paul and Barnabas tried to understand, but it was too fast and the dialect too different to gather much. When the priest finished, the crowd cheered and the people rose to their feet. The priest turned back to Paul and Barnabas with a smile on his face.

"You, speak," he said pointing to Paul. He called to the temple acolytes. The young women quickly brought garlands which they placed on Paul and Barnabas. Then the young men came and lifted Paul and Barnabas to their shoulders and began to carry them into the city.

*

"I met them in Iconium," Timothy explained hurriedly. "They were teaching in the synagogue. They proclaim the Messiah. The Messiah has come to deliver us from our sins. His name is Jesus and we must believe in Him. These men are the servants of God and have the power of God to heal."

"I can walk!" Horace shouted again. "I saw the men come with Timothy. When I heard the man speak about God in heaven, just like Timothy does, I knew that what He said was true. Then he looked at me and told me to stand. So, I did. I did! I walked, and then I ran!" Horace giggled. "I had to come tell you." Horace looked at Vitas. "I had to show you."

"Ahhh!" Rhea cried from inside.

"We have to help your wife," Eunice said as she and Lois both rushed back into the house.

"I didn't thank him," Horace said, suddenly remembering. "We have to go find them."

"Yes, we have to go back and find them," Timothy said. "They don't speak Lyconian. They won't understand what's being said."

"Let's go," Vitas said.

*

They found Paul and Barnabas at the top of the steps in front of the Temple of Zeus, just inside the city gates. Timothy tried to push his way through the crowd, but was getting nowhere. When Horace told the crowd that he was the cripple healed by the men, they ushered the three men to the front. Finally, Timothy, Vitas, and Horace arrived on the steps next to Paul and Barnabas.

"What are you doing here?" Timothy asked them.

"I'm trying to tell them about God, but they don't seem to be listening," Paul answered. "We think they brought us here so the crowd can all hear." The steps of the temple rose up above the crowd. From their place at the top, they could see the entire mass of people.

"No!" Timothy replied. "They brought you here because they think you're gods. They're calling Barnabas Zeus and they're calling you Hermes."

"No!" Paul cried out. He grabbed his clothes at the collar and ripped them. "Timothy, translate for me to the priest. We must make him understand. This madness must not continue."

Paul ran to the priest with Timothy by his side. Timothy translated Paul's words to the priest, "We are not gods. We are men like you."

"Yes," the priest replied to Timothy. "Sometimes the gods appear to us as men. We must offer sacrifices to them. Tell the gods that we will offer these bulls in their names. Today is a great day that the gods have come among us." The priest grabbed Timothy by the shoulders and shook him, "And you are chosen to be the messenger of the gods!"

Timothy translated for Paul and Barnabas the message as quickly as the priest said it. Paul moved in front of the priest and stopped him. "No! We are not gods in the form of men. We are men like you are. I am not Hermes. This man is not Zeus. Do not offer these sacrifices. We come that you might turn from false gods to the living God." Timothy translated the words quickly. Paul turned to the crowd of people. He called to them, pleading with them, "Men, why are you doing this? We also are men, of like nature with you." Timothy moved to Paul's side and called out the translation. "We proclaim to you to turn from these vain things to the living God, who made the heaven and the earth and the sea, and everything that is in them. God in times past allowed all nations to walk in their own ways. Yet He did not leave Himself without witness. He did good and gave us rain from heaven and fruitful seasons to satisfy our hearts with food and gladness."

The priest grabbed Horace by the arm and dragged him before Paul. "I know this man," the priest said. "He has sat on these steps and I have given him food. I had pity on him because he was a cripple. How does he stand and walk before us today?"

Horace answered, "I walk by the faith I have in the God of heaven. Not by the power of Zeus or any other god."

"It is by the power of God in heaven and the name of His Son Jesus Christ that God has healed this man's legs," Paul answered.

"You are gods, and we will offer our sacrifices to you," the priest replied.

"Do not offer sacrifices to us," Barnabas said.

The priest stopped and looked at Barnabas. He began to kneel before him, but Barnabas caught his arm and pulled him to his feet. "I am just a man. You will not offer sacrifices to me or any other god. God has given the only sacrifice needed. Jesus is the sacrifice for the sins of the world."

The sun was high in the sky. Timothy was tired. He had not slept in what felt like days. The sun would soon reach its peak and was beating down on them. He turned to the priest and said, “These men proclaim the one true God of heaven. They do not deceive you or the people. You must listen to them.”

Just then a shout arose from the back of the crowd, near the city gates. “Do not believe these men! They’re liars and thieves!” It was Nathan. Carpus and Micah stood next to him. Several other men scampered out of Nathan's wagon and began pushing through the crowd. Timothy’s heart sunk into his stomach. Timothy watched, unable to do anything as the group of men pressed their way to the front, all the time shouting vile names at Paul and Barnabas.

“These men are wanted criminals,” Carpus said to the priest when he made his way to the steps. “They spread their lies in Antioch and in Iconium. We were to arrest them and kill them this very morning in Iconium. We have men from both Antioch and Iconium to bear witness of these truths. These men are dangerous and must be killed.”

“These men are not Zeus and Hermes?” the priest asked in confusion. “They lie?”

“If they were Zeus or Hermes, they would speak to you directly,” Nathan accused, “but they do not even understand our language, do they?” Nathan shot a look of triumph at Timothy.

“No,” the priest replied. “They speak with a translator.”

“They are liars and charlatans, come to deceive you and steal your wealth,” Carpus cried out to the crowd. “Help us finish what we started in Iconium. The law says they must be killed! We must stone them!”

“Seize them!” Nathan shouted.

“Seize them,” the priest declared.

Pandemonium ensued. The temple acolytes grabbed at Paul and Barnabas. Vitas grabbed Timothy. The crowd began to storm the steps. Timothy and Vitas ducked into an alley that ran beside the temple.

"Where's Horace?" Vitas cried. "Did you see him?"

"We have to go back," Timothy answered. "We have to find Paul and Barnabas."

"We can't go back, they'll take you too," replied Vitas.

"I'm going," Timothy answered and turned back toward the corner of the temple. Just as he did two men burst around the corner and into Timothy knocking them all to the ground. It was Horace and Barnabas.

"Run!" Horace cried out.

"Go!" Barnabas shouted.

Chapter 31

Sacrifice

The crowd dispersed once they realized the man was dead. Carpus watched as several young men, boys that he had seen with Timothy, picked up some of the rocks and hurled them at the corpse. Two of them pick up a large rock that had broken off the steps. They carried it and dropped it on the man's head. Carpus heard a cracking sound.

"That's enough!" he shouted. As he walked over to the body, one of the boys kicked it. There was no movement. "Carry the body out of the city. Dump it where the birds can find it."

"Why should we do that?" Denis replied.

"Because I'll give you this," Carpus said, pulling a large coin from his pocket.

"One for each of us," Kirill answered.

Carpus looked around, there were four of them. "I'll give you one coin now, and one when the work is done. I want him out of our city."

The four looked at each other, then Kirill said, "We'll come to your shop, spice merchant." Carpus tossed the coin to the leader. The boys began tossing rocks off the body, then grabbed the legs and began dragging the body out of town. Carpus watched for a moment, then went to find Nathan, Micah, and the rest of their men. He found Nathan speaking to the priest of Zeus.

"We are sorry that we brought this trouble from Iconium," Nathan said. "Thank you for helping us to resolve this matter."

"And what of the other? The one that we thought was Zeus?" the priest asked.

"I'm sure he's already left for the next town," Carpus replied. "He and the translator will no longer be a problem." Carpus did not wish harm to befall Timothy, regardless of the mistake he had made. He would surface eventually and when he did, Carpus would make him understand his error. "Take this as a token of our appreciation," Carpus said, as he dropped several coins into the priest's hand. "We may serve different gods, but we will leave you in peace as you do the same for us."

"Good day to you," the priest replied and walked back to the temple where he disappeared inside.

"Let's go back to my house," Carpus said to the men.

"Aren't we going to find the other one," Nathan asked. "And the boy that betrayed you."

"Justice has been done today," Carpus stated. "One death is enough to pay the price for their sin. Let us eat and rest." The men murmured their agreement and followed after Carpus as he made his way through the streets. Nathan led the horses and wagon on foot behind them.

*

Timothy and Horace watched from their hiding spot. Once the noise had ceased, they had circled back around. Vitas had taken Barnabas back to his home. Timothy had found a hiding spot on a roof not far from the temple.

"I'm sorry for your friend," Horace said. "I would give my legs back if only he was not dead."

Tears streaked both Timothy and Horace's faces. Timothy watched as Paul's body was dragged from the city by those he had once called friends. A battle raged inside Timothy. He wanted to hate them, hate Carpus and Nathan and all the rest of them, but he knew that it was sin that had driven them. Even now, when his mind screamed that he should hate them, his heart compelled him to forgive them.

"Come, let's go," Horace said. "It doesn't look like they're pursuing us."

"Just a moment longer," Timothy whispered. He watched as Carpus walked off toward his house with the rest of the men from Iconium. "Okay," he said. "We can go now."

They took the alleys back toward Vitas' house, avoiding the main streets in case someone should recognize them. As they stepped into the courtyard, it was clear from their faces that Paul would not be joining them. Barnabas leaned against a barrel on the far side of the courtyard when he saw the look on Timothy's face. Shock covered both their tear-stained faces. Timothy heard the cries of a baby. Vitas stepped out of the house with a small bundle wrapped in clean white cloths.

"It's a girl!" he exclaimed, tears flowing freely down his cheeks. "I'm a father."

Timothy looked at him, "Congratulations! I'm so happy for you."

"Oh, Timothy," Vitas cried. "What are we going to do?"

"We're going to rejoice," Barnabas stated confidently as he stood and wiped the tears from his face. "Today is a great day. It is a day that the Lord has made. He has brought new life to this family. Today we rejoice."

"But, how?" Horace asked. "How can we rejoice, when your friend was just killed."

"We saw them drag his body out of the city," Timothy said somberly.

"Solomon wrote that the day of one's death is better than the day of one's birth," Barnabas replied. He moved toward Vitas. "Today we celebrate both, the birth of your daughter," he said to Vitas, "and the death of my friend and brother. Death is not to be feared, my friends. Paul did not fear death. Our Lord and Savior also died."

"You speak of Jesus?" Lois said, stepping out of the house. Eunice joined her in the courtyard.

"Yes," Barnabas replied. "Have you heard of Him?"

"Only what my grandson said in the few moments he was here earlier," Lois answered.

"Barnabas, this is my grandmother, Lois," Timothy jumped to introduce his family, "and this is my mother, Eunice."

"You have raised a brave man," Barnabas said. "He saved my life and the life of my friend when we were in Iconium. For this, you have my gratitude." He moved to thank the women, but they backed off.

"We have not washed," Eunice said. "We are unclean."

"We are all unclean," Barnabas replied. He turned to them all and said, "From our births, we are all tainted by the curse of sin. In Adam we have inherited sin and in our own flesh we have committed sin. We have all come short of God's glory and His righteousness is not found in anyone. But even in our fallen state, God loves us. He loves each one of His creations. For this reason, God has sent His Son–the Messiah. But the Messiah was not just any man, for no human alone could deliver us from sin. No person could be offered as the sacrifice for the sin of another. Instead, God came to earth Himself as a human. The same as God walked in the garden with Adam, He came and walked among us. As God spoke to Abram, He spoke to us. As God delivered the friends from the fire, He came to deliver us. He lived a perfect, sinless life. He taught us to seek after God. Because our own righteousness is not enough, He taught that we are reconciled to God by God's own righteousness. This righteousness God revealed to us in the person of Jesus Christ.

"The high priest condemned Jesus to death and the Romans crucified him. The religious leaders had rejected Jesus and sought only to kill Him, but God meant it for more. Jesus was offered up as the perfect and final sacrifice for sin. This sacrifice did not cover or hide our sins, as the sacrifices of old have done, but this sacrifice destroyed sin and its power completely. Jesus was convicted of no crime, but they still killed Him. He who had no sin took our sin, so we could be reconciled to God. God's righteousness was made our righteousness. Just as by Adam's disobedience, the many were made sinners, by Jesus' obedience, the many are made righteous."

"The Lord has laid on Him the iniquity of us all," Lois said as a tear fell down her cheek.

"He bore the sin of many and made intercession for the transgressor," Eunice added softly.

"Yes!" Barnabas answered. "As the prophet Isaiah foresaw, Jesus died as the sacrifice for our sins. He took our place and paid our penalty."

"Like the ram," Horace said, "the one that Abraham and Isaac found."

Barnabas looked at Horace, "Exactly. Just as God provided the ram as a substitute for Isaac, Jesus is the substitute for each of us. By His death, He has paid forever the penalty of sin. Only by faith in Jesus is one made right with God. He has given His life as the final ransom to free us from sin. He makes pure that which is unclean. He gives power to those who are weak. He sets right all we have made wrong. He restores honor in place of our shame. All that remains is to call on His name in faith."

"I believe," Timothy declared as he stepped into the center. "Before we arrived back in Lystra, on the road from Iconium, I chose to follow Jesus. I believe Jesus is the Messiah. We have all chosen to trust God, but now God calls us to enter the family of faith. Jesus died as the perfect sacrifice for our sins. We must leave our sin behind and enter into the family of God."

"This has been God's promise from the beginning," Lois said as she wiped back the tears. "That He would forgive our sins. That He would restore our souls. Only God could do this."

"And Jesus is God," Timothy replied.

"Timothy," Lois said, a smile spreading across her face, "I believe. I have awaited the Messiah all my life, I believe." She turned to Barnabas. "I'm an old woman and I have seen my share of folly. Your words speak straight to my heart. What you say about Jesus, He is the promised seed of Eve. I believe that Jesus is the Messiah, sent to destroy sin."

"Call upon the name of the Lord and you will be saved," Barnabas said.

"I call on You, God, to make me whole," Lois said as she lifted her face in prayer. "Cleanse me and give me the righteousness of Jesus in place of my sin."

"God," Horace cried out, "You gave me new legs, now give me new life. I trust in You and Your Son Jesus. He died in my place, for my sin. Thank you."

"Jesus," Eunice prayed to heaven, "I believe You are God and I call on You to save me. I want to be part of the family of faith. Forgive my sin and make me new."

They looked around the courtyard at each other. Their faces were all streaked with tears. Vitas stood by the doorway, rocking his newborn daughter.

Horace looked at Vitas, "Vitas, do you believe?"

"I believe in God," Vitas replied, "but I'm scared. I saw them attack in the market. We barely made it out of there." He looked at Barnabas, "Your friend didn't. Now I have this precious child, and my wife. I don't want to die. I'm sorry, but yours seems to be a religion of death. Your Jesus died and your friend died."

"This is true," Barnabas answered. Then he looked Vitas in the eye, "But the grave could not hold Jesus for long."

Chapter 32

New Life

"What do you mean," Vitas asked, "the grave could not hold Him for long?"

"I mean," Barnabas replied, "Jesus did not stay dead. He arose. Three days His body lay in the grave, but on the third day, He arose. The women who had been closest to Him went to the tomb early the morning after the Sabbath. His body had been laid in a garden tomb, just outside the city. The rulers had placed a guard at the tomb and sealed a large stone in front of the entrance. When the women neared the tomb, they found the stone rolled away and the tomb empty. Angels appeared to them and told them to go tell Jesus' disciples that He had risen. The disciples found the tomb empty except for the linen cloth in which the body had been wrapped. Over the next forty days Jesus appeared many times, teaching and giving evidence of His resurrection. He was seen by Peter and by the twelve. He appeared to over 500 in Galilee, many who are still alive. He appeared to James, His brother, who did not believe before, but who now believes and proclaims salvation in Jesus' name. Then He showed Himself even to those of us in Jerusalem before He ascended into heaven."

"You saw Jesus," Vitas asked, "after He had been killed?"

"Yes," Barnabas replied with a smile shining on His face. "I saw Him with my own eyes and heard Him with my own ears. He showed the healed scars of His death and ate before us. He taught us of the kingdom of God and told us to preach the gospel in His name. He told us to go to the ends of the earth to testify of salvation in His name."

"He ascended into heaven?" Horace asked. "What do you mean by that?"

"I mean," answered Barnabas, "that He rose from the ground and disappeared into the clouds. He returned to the Father."

"I wish I could have seen that," Timothy said.

"I'm happy just being able to walk," Horace replied.

"As we stood watching the sky, two angels appeared and told us that just as Jesus had been taken to heaven, one day, He will come again to gather all who believe," Barnabas added.

"The resurrection at the last day," Lois said.

"Yes," Barnabas replied. "That's what we believe. It's the hope we have that when we die, we too will be given new life. If God can give life to the dead as He did with Jesus and with Lazarus, then we believe He will give us new life after death in the presence of God."

"Lazarus?" Vitas asked. "Who's that?"

"He was a friend of Jesus," Barnabas answered. "Jesus and His disciples often stayed in his home when they came to Jerusalem. Lazarus died just weeks before Jesus was killed. Many said that if Jesus had been there, He could have healed his sickness. But Jesus did not come in time. This was according to His will though, because when Jesus came to the funeral, He raised Lazarus from the dead. He called him out of the grave and Lazarus walked out, risen from the dead and healed of all sickness. Many believed in Jesus because of Lazarus."

"I wish I could see something like that," Vitas said. "If I did, then I could believe."

"Let's go," Lois said as she started for the gate.

"Where are you going?" Timothy called to his grandmother.

"I'm going to meet this friend of yours," she answered, "to see if God is the God of death or of life. You coming?"

Lois was at the gate and out into the street before any of the rest of them could move. Barnabas left first. "Spirit of God, give new life today," he called toward heaven then followed Lois.

Timothy and Horace looked to Vitas. Vitas shrugged, "Let's go." The three men started toward the gate. Vitas still had the baby in his arms.

"Stop!" Eunice shouted. "Give me that baby. She doesn't go anywhere. I'll take her back inside to Rhea." She gently took the infant from his arms, then said, "Go!"

The three friends raced through the streets, chasing after Lois and Barnabas. They found Barnabas at the end of the street. Lois made it to the city gates before the men caught her.

"This way," Timothy called. "They took him out here."

The group made their way down the hill in silence, following the trail of blood. When they arrived at the body, Lois let out a gasp. Horace looked away. Barnabas knelt on the ground next to what remained of his friend. Tears flowed freely down his face. Timothy joined Barnabas on the ground next to the body. One by one, Lois, then Horace, and finally Vitas knelt on the ground as well. Tears filled their eyes. Paul was dead.

"God," Lois cried out to the heavens, "You are the God of Abraham, Isaac, and Jacob. You are my God. Be the God of the living."

Barnabas prayed, "Jesus, O Lord, You are my God. I will exalt You and I will praise Your name. You said that You would swallow death for all time."

"And the Lord God will wipe away tears from all faces," Paul answered. Paul sat up and wiped the dust from his face. He looked at the faces all staring at him. "What happened?"

Barnabas threw his arms around Paul and cried for joy. Lois raised her arms to heaven and shouted praises to God. Timothy could hardly believe what he had just seen. Where moments before had lain a mangled, dead body, now sat the same man he had come to know on the road from Iconium. Horace jumped to his feet and started dancing for joy.

Vitas startled them all when he cried out, "Oh, God! Forgive my unbelief. Cleanse me of sin and make me Yours. My family will not fear death because You are the God who conquers death!"

Barnabas took Paul's face in his hands and looked him in the eyes. "My friend, you were dead. They stoned you on the steps in the city and dragged your body out here for the birds."

"I feel fine," Paul said. He lifted both arms and brushed off the dirt. Then he looked around, "Timothy." Paul smiled as he said the name. Then he spotted Horace. "You're putting those legs to good use," Paul laughed.

"This is my grandmother, Lois," Timothy said. "And that's Horace."

"And my name is Vitas and I believe in Jesus because of you," Vitas interrupted.

"Vitas," Paul took Vitas' outstretched hand. "Timothy told us about you." He stood to his feet. "I'm hungry. You think you can help me out?"

Vitas laughed, "Let's eat!"

*

The sun was beginning to go down as they arrived back at Vitas' house. Vitas called out, "We're back!"

"Hurry, come inside," Rhea called from the house.

Rhea sat reclined on a bed by the fire, holding her baby. Eunice was busily preparing food. She stopped her work as Timothy stepped inside followed by a slightly disheveled, but otherwise perfectly healthy man.

Vitas introduced Paul, "Rhea, Eunice, this is my friend, Paul. He is the evidence of our faith in Jesus Christ. We no longer need to fear."

"Are you okay? Eunice told me everything," Rhea said. A worried look crossed her face. "He was dead?"

"He was," Vitas answered as he knelt beside his wife. "But God has raised him just as Jesus has risen. Jesus is the Messiah that Timothy has told us about. We must believe in Him to be cleansed from our sin."

"I believe," Rhea answered. "I believe."

"Hello!" The call came from the courtyard. Vitas looked around. Everyone was here. He stood and walked toward the door. He stepped outside for a moment, then came back in, followed by four young men.

"Timothy, they say they're friends of yours," Vitas said.

Timothy saw them and jumped at them. Vitas grabbed him and held him back. "They killed Paul! They're the ones that did it," Timothy shouted.

"You're right," Kirill said as they backed toward the door. "You're right. We did. But then we saw you go out to the body." He stopped when he saw Paul. All four stared at Paul, shocked to see him standing on his feet.

Paul walked over to them and said, "Do not be afraid. You have come seeking Jesus. He can give you peace."

"We killed you," Denis said, poking Paul in the shoulder.

"I dropped a rock on your head," Darius stammered.

"You were dead," Jason said.

"What are you doing here?" Timothy asked. His heart was racing.

"We saw you, Timothy," Kirill said. He stepped forward as his courage returned. "We followed you thinking we might capture you and take you to the priest. We watched as you all kneeled around the body. Then you sat up." Kirill placed his hand on Paul's chest.

"We were scared," Denis interjected, "so we ran."

"But I stopped them. I said that we had to follow you," Kirill continued. "I wanted to know what happened."

"We all do," Jason added.

"The food is ready," Eunice called from beside the fire. "Please join us."

"Yes," Vitas said. "Dine at my table. Paul will answer all your questions."

The four newcomers looked around. Timothy had calmed down and gestured for them to stay. Everyone took a seat, forming a semicircle around Paul. As they began to eat, Paul began to explain, "Death comes upon all people because all have sinned against God. Not Zeus or Hermes as the people mistakenly thought we were. I speak of the one true God. The God who has made all that is. You killed me, it's true, but God has given me life. I am here as evidence before you of the power of God. Now, I live by faith in the Son of God, who loved me and gave Himself for me. By the power of the name of Jesus, I live. In Jesus, I am free from the power of sin and of death."

"Timothy," Denis asked, "is this the God that you told us about?"

"It is," Timothy answered. He looked at his friends. He had known them for years and here they sat, ready to hear the message he had prayed they would hear. God had heard his prayer. And now, he too was ready. Timothy spoke the words of God,

"I trust Jesus with my life and you can as well. The power of the resurrected Lord gives us new life, not for this life only, but eternal life with God."

"I don't understand all this," Kirill responded, "but I want what you have. I'll learn whatever you have to teach me, but let me follow your God."

"Turn from your false gods and ask forgiveness in the name of Jesus and you will be saved," Paul said.

Each in turn called on Jesus to save him, first Kirill, then Denis, Jason, and Darius. When they finished, laughter and joy spread around the room. As they ate, Paul, Barnabas, and Timothy took turns retelling the story of their escape from Iconium and their journey to Lystra. The small congregation of believers listened intently as Paul and Barnabas retold the stories of Jesus. As Eunice lit candles and began placing them around the room, a ruckus came from the courtyard.

"Timothy! Timothy! I know you're in there." It was Carpus. The laughter and talking stopped. Timothy looked around to his family and friends, then began to rise.

Vitas grabbed his arm, "No, you stay here." Then Vitas called out to the courtyard, "Timothy's here, but I think you should come inside first."

A moment passed, then Carpus opened the door and stepped inside. "My boy, I don't know what you think you're…." Carpus stood in the doorway with his mouth ajar. His eyes were fixed on the man sitting next to the fire.

"Shut your mouth and come sit down, you old fool," Lois snapped. "It's time you listened to the voice of God."

Chapter 33

New Beginning

Paul rose to his feet and walked to the door. Carpus raised his hand to cover his mouth. Timothy could see the tremor in his hand. As Paul stood before Carpus, he said, "Don't be afraid, friend. What you intended to harm me, God intended it for good."

"Joseph!" Vitas shouted.

"Shhh!" Rhea hushed him.

Vitas looked around sheepishly, "Well, it's from Joseph. Joseph said that to his brothers." Rhea gave him an exasperated look. "Oh, I get it," he said.

"No," Carpus muttered.

"Come, join me by the fire," Paul said to Carpus.

"No," Carpus drew back, "this is wrong. You. I killed you."

Timothy jumped to his feet, "Uncle, look at me. *Look at me.* You did. You killed him. But God has given him new life."

"No, no, no," insisted the old man as he shook his head. He spotted Kirill and the others. He pointed his long finger at them as he shouted, "What did you do? He was dead when you dragged him out!"

"Yes, he was dead," Kirill jumped to his feet. "He was dead until they went out. Then he was alive."

"NO! This *can't* be," Carpus shouted. He pulled away from Timothy and turned to the door to leave.

"YES! In the last days it will be," Barnabas proclaimed. Carpus stopped in his tracks. Barnabas stood next to the fireplace. Everyone stopped talking and looked at Barnabas. Carpus turned. "In the last days," Barnabas repeated, "it will be that I will pour out My Spirit on all flesh. Even on My servants, I will pour out My Spirit. I will work wonders in the heavens and the earth. And whoever calls on the name of the Lord will be saved. I declare unto you," Barnabas said as he looked straight at Carpus, "that name by which we are saved, Jesus of Nazareth. Look! Many signs and wonders testify to the anointing of God. See the cripple who walks." Horace stood to his feet as Barnabas motioned for him to rise. "See the dead brought to life." Barnabas gestured toward Paul. "We are only servants of the Lord, but Jesus did these things and many more.

"Our fathers looked for the Messiah, the One that God promised. They waited for the One who would deliver us from death which is the power and penalty of sin. And when the Messiah came, Jesus was handed over by sinful men to be crucified and killed. But death could not hold Him! It was not possible for death to keep Him because even death bows before the almighty Creator of heaven and earth. God raised up Jesus from the dead, of this I am witness. He is now exalted at the right hand of God, and we have received from the Father His Holy Spirit. It is the Spirit of God that declares to you," Barnabas paused, "that God has made this Jesus, whom you have rejected and killed, both Lord and Messiah."

The entire room was silent. Only the sound of the flame, crackling in the night could be heard. Then Timothy heard sobbing. It was Carpus behind him. At first, a single tear rolled down his cheek, then the floodgates opened. "What should I do?" the old man called out as he fell to his knees.

"Repent and be baptized, every one of you, in the name of Jesus for the forgiveness of sins and you will receive the Spirit of God," Barnabas answered.

"I repent," Carpus pleaded. "I repent of the murder of this servant of God. I repent of my pride and arrogance. For that which I have taken unlawfully, I repent. For the untruths I have told, I repent. For all that I have allowed to blind me, I repent. God forgive me, a sinner. Give me new life with you."

Timothy hugged Carpus. "I knew you would find your way home!"

"Oh, my son," Carpus cried. "Can you ever forgive me? I didn't listen to you until it was too late. You knew. You saw. I don't know how, but you did. Forgive me."

"I love you, Uncle," Timothy replied as he squeezed again.

Carpus turned to Paul, "I…" He began to cry again.

"Anyone that's in Christ is a new person," Paul comforted. "Old things are gone; all things are made new. Christ came to reconcile us, not to count our sin. From now on, we are brothers." The two men clasped arms, then hugged.

"What is the Spirit of God?" Denis asked. "You said the Holy Spirit and the Spirit of God. I don't understand."

"The Holy Spirit was the final gift from Jesus for all who follow Him," Barnabas answered. "Before He ascended to the Father, Jesus commanded us to take this gospel throughout the world. He told us to preach repentance and the remission of sins in His name to all nations. He said that we would testify of Him even to the ends of the earth, but that we would begin in Jerusalem. We were to wait there until He baptized us with the Holy Spirit. The Spirit was to give us God's power from on high. So, we stayed together in the city. On Pentecost, the fiftieth day after the Passover, the Holy Spirit fell on us. It came with the sound of a mighty rushing wind, and we saw it as a tongue of fire above every person. The entire house of Israel gathered in Jerusalem that day to celebrate the giving of the law. God gave us the power to proclaim the fulfillment of the law. We went out into the streets and preached Jesus to all. People from every nation heard us that day in Jerusalem. Peter stood before them and declared Jesus to be the fulfillment of God's promise to our fathers, much as I just said to Carpus. And like Carpus, many of our brothers repented and received the word of God."

"All who trust Jesus as their Savior are filled with the Holy Spirit," Paul added. "He now dwells in you, to guide and teach you. You must listen to Him and follow His lead."

"I have the Spirit of God inside me?" Kirill asked.

"Can't you feel it?" asked Denis. "I'm not afraid anymore. It's like, I don't know, like a clear, peaceful sky after a long storm. That's how my heart feels."

"You can't see Him," Paul answered, "but He will give you peace, and love, and hope, and joy."

Horace spoke, "You said something about being baptized? What's that?"

"It's a public sign of your faith," Paul answered. "It shows your repentance to those around you. We baptize you into the water and then raise you up out of it as a sign of your obedience."

"It also shows our identification with Christ as you are buried in the water and risen to new life," Barnabas added. "Is there water around here, a lake or a river?"

"There's a small river just southeast of town, on the road to Derbe," Vitas answered. "Will you baptize us?"

"Yes," Barnabas answered. "We can go first thing in the morning."

"Can we go tonight?" Horace asked.

"It's supposed to be a testimony to others, right?" Timothy asked.

"Yes, it signifies to others the faith in your heart," Paul answered.

"Then let's wait till morning, Horace," Timothy said. "We can all go out together so the whole city can see."

"Yeah, that sounds good," Vitas added.

"I like that," Horace replied.

*

No one returned home that night. They sat around the fire until morning as Paul and Barnabas taught them. By morning the church was ready to baptize their newest members into the body of Christ. Timothy, Lois, and Eunice led the procession through town. Vitas and Horace helped Rhea with the baby. Vitas had insisted that Rhea remain at home, but she said that she had already missed Paul's resurrection, she wasn't missing this. Carpus walked with Paul and Barnabas, one on each side. Kirill, Denis, Jason, and Darius followed in the back, calling out to the city to wake and to hear the word of the Lord. As they walked past Carpus' house, he called for Hannah. A moment later she appeared followed by Nathan, Micah and the rest from Iconium. Carpus took Hannah by the hand and the party continued out of town as Nathan and Micah stood dumbfounded at the gate.

When they arrived at the river, Paul and Barnabas led them into the water. They baptized each one in turn. By the time they had finished, many had followed from town to see the spectacle. Denis stood pleading with his family to call on the name of Jesus. Nathan and Micah were nowhere to be seen, but two of the others from Iconium had followed and Carpus was now testifying to them. Lois and Eunice were sitting under the shade of a tree with Hannah and several other women explaining the forgiveness of sins. Kirill, Jason, and Darius were calling to others to come closer to the river to hear the message of salvation.

Paul turned to Timothy, “We’ll see you again when we return.”

“You’re leaving?” Timothy replied, shocked at Paul’s statement.

“We’ll be back,” Barnabas answered. “But even if we don’t make it, you’ll be fine. You have each other and the Holy Spirit. God’s mission does not stop, so neither does ours. We must continue to preach the name of Jesus until all have heard. Lystra is only the beginning, your beginning.”

“But where are you going?” Timothy asked. He looked at Paul and Barnabas. How had he not seen their packs on their backs as they left town?

“Derbe,” Horace replied. He too had a pack. “I’m taking them to meet the rest of my family back in Derbe. When they see me walk into town, they’ll all believe in Jesus.” Horace did a little jig, laughing and rejoicing at the goodness of God.

“We’ll be okay,” Vitas said as he came to stand beside Timothy. Rhea stood next to Vitas with the baby in her arms. “We can’t keep them to ourselves, there are too many people that still need to hear the gospel message. We can manage around here. After all, you’re still my favorite storyteller, but now you know the end of the story. We’ll tell everybody in town until they’ve all trusted Jesus.”

“Do you really have to go?” Timothy asked, but he knew in his heart that Vitas was right. The gospel must be proclaimed. Vitas would help him to do it here in Lystra, but Horace was right to take Paul and Barnabas to Derbe.

“We'll return after we preach the gospel in Derbe, if we’re able,” Paul said. “If not, I’ll write letters, so watch for messengers.”

Barnabas, Paul, and Horace said their goodbyes, then crossed the river and started down the road toward Derbe. Timothy crossed the river with them and said a final goodbye.

"I'm glad I knocked on your door."

"I am too," Barnabas answered.

"You followed the Spirit of God," Paul replied. "Look at what God can do when you answer His call." Timothy looked across the river. "Repentance and remission of sin has been proclaimed here because you answered the call of God. Who knows, maybe someday God will send you even farther." Paul embraced Timothy and prayed, "God, fill this young man with Your words to declare Your name to his people both here and in regions beyond."

Timothy watched as they started down the road. Horace was already asking them questions. Timothy smiled. He wished he could be going also. He turned back and crossed the river. Vitas met him.

"Time to eat?"

"If we're serving bread of life and living water," Timothy responded as he looked toward Lystra, "I think there's a lot of people ready to eat."

Chapter 34

The Seed

"And then what happened?"

Timothy scanned the courtyard. The summer sun shone brightly above them. He had spent so much time in this home. He saw the room that he had helped Vitas build so many years ago. He smiled that it was still there. The house had not changed much since he had last been here, but the people had gotten older. Timothy saw Kirill, Denis, and Darius, each with his wife and children. Jason had moved to Iconium and was part of the church there. Carpus and Hannah sat in the front. They had both become frail with age, but he could still see the kindness in her eyes and the joy in his. God had changed Carpus completely. He still dominated every conversation, but now he spoke only of Jesus. Many were here today because of him. Several other faces that Timothy did not recognize sat before him as well. Men, women, and children all listening as he told the story of everything that had happened.

Vitas sat beside Timothy. Vitas had aged with grace, or so he had said last night. The truth was that God had blessed him beyond measure. Seven children called him father, but the rest of these gathered in his house called him pastor and friend. Timothy's attention turned back to the young lady that had asked the question. She sat directly before him. He remembered the day she was born. How had she grown so fast? Had he been gone that long?

"And then you started to cry," Vitas joked. Everyone laughed.

"*Papà*," she fussed. Vitas reached down and took her hand. She smiled and his face radiated love. She was his firstborn. Born the same day salvation came to Lystra, Vitas and Rhea had named her after the foreigner who left her gods and her family to follow the God of heaven and join the family of God.

"Ruth, you know what happened next," Vitas answered. "I've told you this story a thousand times."

"But I want to hear Uncle Timothy tell it," she answered. "He tells it so much better than you," she answered with a mischievous grin. Again, everyone laughed.

"If you must know," Timothy answered, "we began to gather the harvest, your father and I, along with Carpus, Kirill, Denis, Jason, and Darius." Timothy looked to each man as he mentioned their names. "Not the harvest of grain that stood in the fields, but the harvest of souls that lived in the city. God added many to our numbers that day. It is a harvest that continues even to this day. It is the work that we are each called to do.

"The Lord told the story of a sower. The sower went out into the field to spread the seed. He cast the seed far and wide across the field. Some of the seeds fell on the path and birds came to eat it. Other seeds fell on rocky ground. These sprang up, but because they were shallow and without root, they withered under the heat of the sun. Some seeds fell among thorns and were choked out because of the weeds. Yet other seeds fell on good ground where it brought forth grain to eat.

"Jesus also gave the explanation of this story. He said that the seed is the Word of God. The ground is the one that hears the Word. Some will hear the gospel, but the evil one will come and quickly snatch it away."

"I was once like this," Kirill said. "When Timothy first came to tell me about God, I mocked him and could not accept his words."

"Yes," Timothy continued. "But I'm so glad you did accept God's word. Others will hear the truth and accept it, but when they face persecution, they fall away. How many of us have seen those who want to follow, but have fallen from the Way because of the trials that came?" A small murmur of agreement arose from the crowd. "Still others hear the Word of God and cannot grow because they are more concerned with the cares of this life than the things of God. Matters of family and friends, wealth and health, work and food easily draw us away from the work of heaven. Yet some will hear the word and spring forth to life and produce fruit for the kingdom of heaven."

"If the seed is the Word of God," Ruth asked, "and the ground is the one that hears the Word, who is the sower? Is it Jesus?"

"No," Timothy replied. "You are the sower. I am the sower. Each of us is the sower. At one time, we were each the ground that received the seed. Some of us received the gospel with joy. Others refuse the message until, at last, the Spirit convicts them of sin and they repent. But when the seed takes root in our heart, and we begin to bear fruit, we become the sower ourselves. I cannot reproduce anything of myself, but I must plant the seed in another. It is the gospel of Christ that gives life. I must cast the seed so that others might grow."

"Do we cast the seed only on the good ground?" asked one of the people Timothy didn't recognize.

"How many of you were once the rocky ground?" Timothy asked. "How many were ground filled with thorns? We must cast the seed to every ground because Jesus died to pay the penalty of sin for all people. Some may complain that they can't find good ground in which to plant their seed. I ask you if a man inherits land filled with rocks, does he leave the ground as it is? No, he labors many days to remove the rocks from the ground. He pulls the thorns from the ground and brings water to the land. We must labor the same for God as we would for a dry piece of land."

"And what if we tire in our labors?" another called out. "There are so many that oppose God both in our own city and in the lands around us."

"Then we endure," Timothy replied. "Does the farmer not tire of the summer heat? If he quits because the sun is too hot, then he misses the harvest. Don't grow weary in doing good, for in due season we will reap, if we don't give up. The day is coming when our Lord will return. Jesus told a second story about a man who planted a field of wheat. When the shoots began to spring from the ground, there were weeds also among them. The man's servants asked if they should gather the weeds. He said to leave them until the harvest when it would be easier to separate the good from the bad. If they gathered the weeds now, they risked destroying the good with the bad.

"In this world there are both sons of God and sons of the devil," Timothy continued. "We must continue about the business of God, but know that the sons of wickedness will oppose you. But it is for them that we remain. We share the gospel message to open their eyes and to turn them from darkness to light. We preach Christ to deliver them from the power of Satan to God. We testify of the Spirit in our lives that they may receive forgiveness of sins and join in the inheritance among those who are sanctified by faith. Don't give up because our work is hard. It is hard, but the reward is sweet. Proclaim the righteousness of Christ because the day will come when God will send His angels to gather the harvest. All those who are of the devil will be delivered to fire and everlasting destruction, but those who are named in Christ will be gathered to God in His everlasting rest.

"God is good, and He desires all people to repent of sin and to come to Him. Hear His voice as He speaks to your heart. Allow the seed of the gospel to grow within you. I implore you today, be reconciled to God. Call on the name of the Lord today. Do not delay for soon the harvest will come."

Cries of "Amen" sprang up from around the courtyard. The congregation rose as one, then Timothy could hear Rhea's voice from the back. She began singing in a soft voice, "I will exalt You, my God and my King. I will bless Your name forever. Every day I will bless Your name forever." As the rest joined in the song, Timothy remembered the day his mother had taught Rhea that song. His heart swelled with joy seeing how God had answered his prayer for Lystra.

"Thank you, God," Timothy prayed, "for Your salvation. Thank you for bringing salvation to all who call on the name of Jesus."

Chapter 35

Grand Narrative

Before time, space, or matter,
before the earth, moon, or sun,
before there was man, there was God.
God exists and He exists without beginning.
God was not made by anyone or anything.
He is the One that made everything.
He created time, space, and matter.
He made the universe and all that is in it.
He made the sun and the earth to go 'round it.
He made the oceans and the seas and the rivers and the lakes.
He made the mountains and the plains and the deserts and the swamps.
Then He filled the earth with all kinds of life.
Animals like
elephants and kangaroos,
camels and horses,
dogs and cats.
He even made the trees and plants;
potatoes and peas,
carrots and beans,
cucumbers, cherries, and strawberries!
But God did not stop there.

You see, God is a being, three-in-one.
God the Father, God the Son, and the Spirit of God.
Together they existed in eternity.
A community of love that now wanted to grow.
So, the capstone of creation, the last, missing piece,
was to make man in God's own image.
Two He created, Adam and Eve.
Man and woman, together to be.
They were given the reins to this brand-new land.
"Be fruitful and multiply, replenish the earth.
Just one rule is all We have.
Don't eat from this tree,
its knowledge will bring
death, destruction, and misery."
A perfect world God had created.
A world without sin or death.
A world where His power could be seen and felt.
But above all, the one thing God wanted,
Now, there was love going out.
Love being given, first from God to man,
then by Adam and Eve, to God from man.
But alas, this is no fairy tale.
It's not once upon a time, nor happily ever after.
This is real.
They were real.
They sinned.
And they fell.
The one thing God said, "Don't do!" They did.
They disobeyed.
They ate.
And then they hid.
God found them and said,
"Because of your sin, death enters this world."

The cost of sin is death, so by man, death entered the world.
A lamb gave its life to cover their sin.
But the price was not paid, just hid.
The world had been ruined because of the fall.
The entrance of sin and death changed it all.
Sickness and pain,
sorrow and loss
now lived among us.
But, "One day,
death dies,
sin loses,
love wins,"
God promised.
Time passed, man grew.
Across the face of the earth man spread his seed.
He built cities, he built walls.
He told himself that he alone was god.
Man turned his back on the love of God.
In his own power, in his own might, man did it all and continued to die.
But despite man's sin, and the choices he made,
God chose to love man and called one out by name.

"Abram come out!"

God chose this one man, this man, and his wife,
to be a great nation, a people, a light.
In a world dark with sin, God's love shone bright.
He gave them a son when they were old.
Isaac was the son God foretold.
He brought them laughter. He brought them joy.
Then Isaac's son Jacob, his second born boy.

From Jacob's twelve boys a nation was formed,
the people God promised now was born.

Israel.
The people of God.
The light in this world.
God spoke to His people,
He gave them His word.
They did as commanded,
obeyed what they heard.
Until they didn't.
Sometimes they heard and rejected God's word
and chased after idols they saw in the world.
They sinned and they fell.
But then turned back to God
where forgiveness was found
in the lamb's shed blood.
See, sin had its price once again.
For every sin there is death.
The lamb's blood would cover their sin.
Cover and hide, but not take away the debt that was owed.
Then once again off to the lusts of the flesh,
the lusts of the eyes, and pride of life.
In these they found but a moment of joy,
then slaves they were made because of this choice.
But God sent his people first judges, then kings,
men who would lead them toward God, to do the right thing.
Some kings chose God and the people were led
to be the bright light God wanted, but then
others chose evil and the name of God
was dirtied and sullied and despised by men.

But faithful prophets who loved and served God
arose to proclaim, "This is the word of the Lord.
Turn from your sins, honor your God.
Obey the commands and reap the rewards.
See if He won't deliver you now
from the burden of sin that is weighing you down.
Know that our God, He is faithful and true.
He promised a way to make all things new.
A Savior will come. A virgin give birth.
And that child will deliver the earth
from the sin and death that enslaves us all.
He'll forgive us and heal us," all this the prophets called.
The message of truth Israel had,
but after false gods the people ran.
In bondage and slavery, not just to sin,
Israel was carried away from the land.
Out in the world their light began to spread,
the nation remembered God's original plan.
A city on a hill, a light to all,
through this family would come God's blessing to all.
Back to the land the remnant went
and there they would wait
and wait
and wait.

Four hundred years God's voice fell silent.
No message.
No word.
No prophet.
No promise.
Then God....

...Then God flipped the whole world on its head.
God, who at various times had spoken through prophets and priests and judges and kings, chose Himself to speak.
So as the prophets foretold,
from the seed of Abram,
the virgin gave birth,
a child was born,
and His name was Emanuel.
God with us.
The Author had become a character, the Creator was made like us.
One hundred percent God, yet one hundred percent man.
He did not come as King or Master,
He came as Servant and Friend.
He, who was not bound by time, space, or matter,
humbled Himself to live life as a man.
They called Him Jesus.
He laughed and He cried.
He feasted and hungered.
Yet unlike everyone who has ever lived,
He remained completely obedient unto God.
Though He was tempted,
He lived a perfect life without sin.
Everywhere He went, people followed.
They came to see Him,
to hear Him,
to touch Him.
In turn He taught us how to live.
He showed grace and love, mercy and truth.
He forgave us our sin and to prove He could do it,
He healed the lame, gave sight to the blind,

made whole the leper and fed the child.
Many followed the Christ, the One that God sent.
In Him they placed faith, for this life and next.
But others turned their backs on Christ,
In protest they grew louder and louder until one night
when they took Him and beat Him. They mocked Him
and said,
"No man can be God. We choose Barabas instead."
The Romans took Him and placed Him suspended between
heaven and earth where all could see.
There on the cross Jesus suffered and died.
The Creator of all gave His own life.

Had evil triumphed? Was that the end?
Did this spell defeat? But then....
Sin demands death; Jesus knew no sin.
Man's place had God taken, He paid my sin.
Three days was He dead.
Three days did He lay in a grave
that no longer could His glory contain.
He arose! He arose! Hallelujah! Christ arose!
Jesus, our Sacrifice, our Hero, our Savior arose!
God's plan of redemption was finally done.
The battle of sin and death had been won.
Death had been killed
Sin's power, destroyed.

Jesus walked and He talked with His followers and then
He left them to go back to heaven again.
He told them to go with the message of hope,
to proclaim salvation in Jesus alone.
To all the world a blessing to be,
this Son of Man,

seed of Abraham,
promised Messiah,
Jesus was He!

This message we spread till all have heard,
every people and tribe and tongue and nation.
He told them He's coming again one day
to gather His own to a home far away.
He will make all things new, right all the wrong.
Sin and death and fear will be gone.
As King He will reign over creation made new,
just as He promised and said He would do.

God who has made us, and loves us, and calls us by name,
now calls you to follow the path He has made.
Salvation is offered completely free,
but only in Jesus forgiven we'll be.
Run away, hide like Adam and Eve,
but sin's cost is still death and guilty are we.
Payment in full must be made,
separated from God in hell is choice A.
Choice B is forgiven and free,
the payment paid full on Calvary's tree.
God loves you and wants you to believe.
So, choose Him, trust Him, follow, and see
that God's love is the power you need.
And as we repeat this story of God,
the message of hope proclaims life brand new for anyone.

Appendix

The motivation for this book has always been to draw people to the Bible and the God that is revealed therein. Each chapter of this book draws inspiration from the Bible. This appendix is not intended to be an exhaustive list of all the Bible has to say on the matters discussed within this book; it is a list of the verses that inspired the stories in it. My prayer and hope is that you find as much treasure in the pages of Scripture as I have.

Chapter 1
Creation - Genesis 1-2
Other verses - James 1:17

Chapter 2
The Fall - Genesis 2-3
Other verses - Deuteronomy 32:39; Psalm 23:4

Chapter 3
Cain and Abel - Genesis 4:1-16; Hebrews 11:4
Other verses - Romans 5:12-21; Psalm 51:5; Proverbs 3:5-7

Chapter 4
The Flood - Genesis 6-9; Hebrews 11:7
Other verses - Jeremiah 18:1-4; Psalm 22:2-5

Chapter 5
God's Promise to Abraham- Genesis 12:1-3, 13:14-18, 15:1-6, 16:1-17:27, 21:1-8

Chapter 6
Abraham and Isaac - Genesis 22:1-19, 21:11-13, 15:6; Hebrews 11:17-19

Chapter 7
Looking for Joseph's Brothers - Genesis 37
Other verses - Ezekiel 11:19, 36:26

Chapter 8
Bad Times in Egypt - Genesis 39
Other verses - Leviticus 19:18, 33-34

Chapter 9
Raised to Power - Genesis 41

Chapter 10
Making Things Right - Genesis 42-46

Chapter 11
The Plagues and Passover - Exodus 1-13
Other verses - Deuteronomy 6:5

Chapter 12
Journey in the Desert - Exodus 15:23-27, 16, 17:5-7 Numbers 11, 21:5-9

Chapter 13
Joshua at Jericho - Joshua 5:13-6:27
Other verses - 2 Samuel 22:29-33; Psalm 18:28-32

Chapter 14
Gideon - Judges 6-7

Chapter 15
Samson - Judges 13-16

Chapter 16
Saul and David - 1 Samuel 8-10, 13, 16-17

Chapter 17
Showdown on Mt. Carmel - 1 Kings 18:17-40
Other verses - Psalm 145:1-2; 127:3; Numbers 6:24-26

Chapter 18
Jonah - Jonah 1-4
Other verses - Psalm 34:4-7; Isaiah 42:6, 49:6

Chapter 19
Daniel's Diet - Daniel 1
Other verses - Proverbs 20:1

Chapter 20
Fiery Furnace - Daniel 3
Other verses - Genesis 3:19

Chapter 21
Lions' Den - Daniel 6

Chapter 22
John in the Jordan - Matthew 3; Mark 1:1-11; Luke 3:1-22; John 1:6-8, 15-34; Acts 13:24-25

Chapter 23
Introducing Jesus - Luke 4; Acts 13
Other verses - Acts 14:1-5

Chapter 24
Nicodemus - John 2:13-3:21
Other verses - Acts 14:6

Chapter 25
Forgiven - Matthew 9:1-8; Mark 2:1-12; Luke 5:17-26

Chapter 26
Living Water - John 4

Chapter 27
Bread of Life - John 6

Chapter 28
Rich People - Luke 18:18-30, 19:1-10

Chapter 29
Lost Things - Luke 15

Chapter 30
Lystra - Acts 14:8-19a

Chapter 31
Crucifixion - Matthew 26-27; Mark 14-15 Luke 22-23; John 18-19
Other verses - Acts 14:19b; Ecclesiastes 7:1; Romans 3, 5; 2 Corinthians 5; Isaiah 53

Chapter 32
Resurrection - Matthew 28; Mark 16 Luke 24; John 20-21; Acts 1
Lazarus - John 11, 12:1, 9-11;

Other verses - Acts 14:20a; Isaiah 25:1,8; Romans 5:12; Galatians 2:20

Chapter 33
Pentecost - Acts 1-2
Great Commission - Matthew 28:18-20; Mark 16:15; Luke 24:46-49; John 20:21; Acts 1:8
Other verses - Genesis 50:20; Joel 2; 2 Corinthians 5; Acts 14:20b

Chapter 34
The Seed - Matthew 13
Other verses - Psalm 145:1-2

About the Author

Eric S. Schrock is an American missionary, living in Romania for the past fifteen years. He is the planter and pastor of a church in the heart of Transylvania. Eric obtained a masters degree in Global Studies from Liberty University in 2019, and holds a BA in Bible from Pensacola Christian College (2001). He and his wife are proud parents of three children, to whom this book is dedicated.

If you enjoyed this book, please consider leaving an online review. The author would appreciate reading your thoughts.

Visit the website at +

Subscribe to the newsletter at

You can also follow the author on social media
Instagram:
Twitter:
FaceBook:

About the Publisher

Sulis International Press publishes select fiction and nonfiction in a variety of genres under four imprints: Riversong Books, Sulis Academic Press, Sulis Press, and Keledei Publications.

For more, visit the website at
https://sulisinternational.com

Subscribe to the newsletter at
https://sulisinternational.com/subscribe/

Follow us on social media
https://www.facebook.com/SulisInternational
https://twitter.com/Sulis_Intl
https://www.pinterest.com/Sulis_Intl/
https://www.instagram.com/sulis_international/

Made in the USA
Monee, IL
06 February 2022

90352167R00144